Marie Corelli

Barabbas - A Dream of the World's Tragedy

Vol. II

Marie Corelli

Barabbas - A Dream of the World's Tragedy
Vol. II

ISBN/EAN: 9783744789998

Printed in Europe, USA, Canada, Australia, Japan

Cover: Foto ©Andreas Hilbeck / pixelio.de

More available books at **www.hansebooks.com**

BARABBAS

A DREAM OF THE WORLD'S TRAGEDY

BY

MARIE CORELLI

AUTHOR OF
'THELMA' 'A ROMANCE OF TWO WORLDS' 'ARDATH'
'VENDETTA!' 'WORMWOOD: A DRAMA OF PARIS'
'THE SOUL OF LILITH'

IN THREE VOLUMES

VOL. II

Methuen & Co.
18 BURY STREET, LONDON, W.C.
1893

BARABBAS

A DREAM OF THE WORLD'S TRAGEDY

——•——

XVIII

SHRIEKS and groans,—confusion and clamour,—
wild shouts for help,—wilder cries for light,—
and the bewildering, maddening knowledge that
numbers of reckless terrified human beings were
rushing hither and thither, unseeingly and distractedly,
—these were the first results of that abrupt descent
of black night in bright day. 'Light! Give us
light, O God!' wailed a woman's voice, piercing
through the dismal dark; and the frantic appeal,
'Light! light!' was re-echoed a thousand times by
the miserable, desperate, wholly panic-stricken crowd.
To and fro wandered straggling swarms of men and
women, touching each other, grasping each other,

5

but unable to discern the faintest outline of each other's forms or features. Some sought to grope their way down the hill, back to the city,—some wrestled furiously with opposing groups of persons in their path,—others, more timorous, stayed where they were, weeping, shrieking, striking their breasts and repeating monotonously, 'Light,—light! O God of our fathers, give us light!'

But no answer to their supplications came from the sable pall that solemnly loomed above them, for now not even the lightning threw a chance spear across the clouds, though with incessant, unappeased ferocity the thunder roared, or rolling to a distance muttered and snarled. A soldier of more self-possession and sense than his fellows managed after a little while to strike a light from flint and steel, and as soon as the red spark shone, a hundred hands held out to him twigs and branches that they might be set on fire and so create a blazing luminance within the heavy gloom. But scarcely had a branch or two been kindled, when such a shriek went up from those on the edge of the crowd as froze the blood to hear.

'The faces of the dead!' they cried—'The dead

are there,—there, in the darkness! Shut them out! Shut them out! They are all dead men!'

This mad outcry was followed by the screams of women, mingled with hysterical bursts of laughter and weeping, many persons flinging themselves face forward on the ground in veritable agonies of terror, —and the soldier who had struck the light dropped his implements, paralysed and aghast. The kindled branches fell and sputtered out,—and again the un-natural midnight reigned, supreme, impermeable. There was no order left; the soldiery were scattered; the mob were separated into lost and wandering sections; and 'Light! light!' was the universal moan. Truly, in that sepulchral blackness, they were 'the lost sheep of the house of Israel,' ignorantly and foolishly clamouring for 'light!' when the one and only Light of the World was passing through the 'Valley of the Shadow,' and all Nature in the great name of God, was bound to go with Him! The atmosphere lost colour, — the clouds thundered,— earth trembled,—the voices of birds and animals were mute,—the trees had ceased to whisper their leafy loves and confidences,—the streams stopped in their

silver-sounding flow,—the sun covered its burning
face,—the winds paused on their swift wings,—and
only Man asserted, with puny groans and tears, his
personal cowardice and cruelty in the presence of the
Eternal. But at this awful moment the powers of
heaven were deaf to his complaining, and his craven
cries for help were vain. Our shuddering planet,
stricken with vast awe and wonder to its very centre,
felt with its suffering Redeemer the pangs of dissolution, and voluntarily veiled itself in the deep
shadow of death,— a shadow that was soon to be
lifted and gloriously transformed into light and life
immortal !

The heavy moments throbbed away,—moments
that seemed long as hours,—and no little gleaming
rift broke the settled and deepening blackness over
Calvary. Many of the people, giving way to despair,
cast themselves down in the dust and wept like
querulous children, — others huddled themselves
together in seated groups, stunned by fright into
silence, — a few howled and swore continuously,—
and all the conflicting noises merging together,
suggested the wailing of lost beings in spiritual

torment. All at once the strong voice of the high-priest Caiaphas, hoarse with fear, struck through the gloom.

'People of Jerusalem!' he cried—'Kneel and pray! Fall down before the God of Abraham, of Isaac and of Jacob, and entreat Him that this visitation of storm and earthquake be removed from us! Jehovah hath never deserted His children, nor will He desert them now, though it hath pleased Him to afflict us with the thunders of His wrath! Be not afraid, O ye chosen people of the Lord, but call upon Him with heart and voice to deliver us from this darkness! For we have brought His indignation upon ourselves, inasmuch as we have suffered the false prophet of Galilee to take His Holy Name in vain, and He doth show us by His lightnings the fiery letter of His just displeasure. And whereas these shadows that encompass us are filled perchance with evil spirits who come to claim the soul of the boastful and blasphemous Nazarene, I say unto ye all, cover yourselves and pray to the God of your fathers, O sons and daughters of Jerusalem, that He may no longer be offended,—that He may hear your supplications

in the time of trouble, and bring you out of danger
into peace!'

His exhortation, though pronounced in tremulous
tones, was heard distinctly, and had the desired
effect. With one accord the multitude fell on their
knees, and in the thickening shadows that enveloped
them began to pray as they were told,—some silently,
some aloud. Strange it was to hear the divers con-
trasting petitions that now went muttering up to the
invisible Unknown ;—Latin tongues against Hebrew
and Greek,—appeals to Jupiter, Mercury, Diana and
Apollo, mingling with the melancholy chant and
murmur of the Jews.

'Our God, God of our fathers, let our prayer come
before Thee! Hide not Thyself from our supplica-
tion! We have sinned,—we have turned aside from
Thy judgments, And it hath profited us naught!
Remember us, O God, and be merciful! Consume
us not with Thy just displeasure! Be merciful and
mindful of us for blessing! Save us unto life! By
Thy promise of salvation and mercy, Spare us and
be gracious unto us, O God!'

And while they stammered out the broken phrases,

half in hope, half in fear, the thunder, gathering
itself together like an army of war - horses and
chariots, for sole reply crashed down upon them in
the pitchy darkness with a fulminating ferocity so
relentless and awful, that the voices of all the people,
Jews and aliens alike, died away in one long quaver-
ing, helpless human wail.   Their prayers sank to
affrighted whispers,—and the thunder still pelting
in angry thuds through the dense air, was as the
voice of God, pronouncing vast and unimaginable
things.

Meanwhile, as already described, Barabbas had
rushed towards Judith Iscariot just as the darkness
fell,—and when the blinding vapours enveloped him
he still kept on his course, striking out both arms
as he ran that they might come first in contact with
the woman he loved.   He had calculated his distance well, — for presently, his outstretched hands,
groping heedfully up and down in the sombre murk,
touched a head that came to about the level of his
knee,—then folds of silk, — then the outline of a
figure that was huddled up on the ground quite
motionless.

'Judith!—Judith!' he whispered—'Speak! Is it thou?'

No answer came. He stooped and felt the crouching form; here and there he touched jewels,—and then he remembered she had worn a dagger at her girdle. Cautiously passing his arms about, he found the toy weapon hanging from the waist of this invisible woman-shape, and realised, with a thrill of comfort, that he was right,—it was Judith he touched, —but she had evidently fainted from terror. He caught her, clasped her, lifted her up, and supported her against his breast, his heart beating with mingled despair and joy. Chafing her cold hands, he looked desperately into the dense obscurity, wondering whether he could move from the spot without stumbling against one at least of those three terrible crosses which he knew must be very near. For Judith had stood directly beneath that on which the wondrous 'Nazarene' was even now slowly dying, and she would scarcely have had time to move more than a few steps away when the black eclipse had drowned all things from sight. He, Barabbas, might at this moment be within an arm's length of that strange 'King' whose crown was of thorns,—an awful and awe-inspiring idea that filled him with horror. For, to be near that mysterious Man of Nazareth,—to know that he might almost touch His pierced and bleeding feet,—to feel perchance, in the horrid gloom, the sublime and mystic sorrow of His eyes,—to hear the parting struggle of His breath,—this would be too difficult, too harrowing, too overwhelming for the endurance or fortitude of one who knew himself to be the guilty sinner that should have suffered in the place of the Innocent and Holy. Seeking thus to account to his own mind for the tempestuous emotions which beset him, Barabbas moved cautiously backward, not forward, bearing in his recollection the exact spot in which he had seen Judith standing ere the black mists fell ; and, clasping her firmly, he retreated inch by inch, till he thought he was far enough removed from that superhuman Symbol which made its unseen Presence all-dominant even in the darkness. Then he stopped, touching with gentle fingers the soft scented hair that lay against his breast, while he tried to realise his position. How many a time he would have given his life to have held Judith thus familiarly close to his heart!—but now,—now there was something dreary, weird and terrible, in what, under other circumstances, would have been unspeakable rapture. Impossible, in this black chaos, to see the features or the form of her whom he embraced; only by touch he knew her; and a faint chill ran through him as he supported the yielding supple shape of her in his arms;—her silken robe, her perfumed hair,—the cold contact of the gems about her,—these trifles repelled him strangely, and a sense of something sinful oppressed his soul. Sin and he were old friends,—they had rioted together through many a tangle of headstrong passion,—why should he recoil at Sin's suggestions now? He could not tell,—but so it was;—and his brain swam with a nameless giddy horror, even while he ventured, trembling, to kiss the unseen lips of the creature he had but lately entirely loved, and now partly loathed.

And,—as he kissed her she stirred,—her body quivered in his hold,—consciousness returned, and in a moment or two she lifted herself upright. Sighing heavily, she murmured like one in a dream—

'Is it thou, Caiaphas?'

A fierce pang contracted the heart of the unhappy man who loved her, — he staggered, and
almost let her fall from his embrace. Then,
controlling his voice with an effort, he answered
hoarsely—

'Nay,—it is I,—Barabbas.'

'Thou!' and she flung one arm about his neck
and held him thus entwined—'Thou wert ever brave
and manful!—save me, my love, save me! Take me
out of this darkness,—there must be light in the
city,—and thou art fearless and skilful enough to
find a way down this accursèd hill.'

'I cannot, Judith!' he answered, his whole frame
trembling at the touch of her soft caressing arm,—
'The world is plunged in an impenetrable night,—
storm and upheaval threaten the land, — the city
itself is blotted out from view. The people are at
prayer; none dare move without danger,—there is
no help for it but to wait, here where we are, till
the light cometh.'

'What, thou art coward after all!' exclaimed
Judith, shaking herself free from his clasp—'Thou

fool! In the city, lamps can be lit, and fires kindled, and we be spared some measure of this gloom. If thou wert brave,—and more than all, if thou didst love me,—thou would'st arouse thy will, thy strength, thy courage,—thou would'st lead me safely through this darkness as only love can lead,—but thou art like all men, selfish and afraid!'

'Afraid! Judith!' His chest heaved,—his limbs quivered. 'Thou dost wrong me!—full well thou knowest thou dost wrong me!'

'Prove it then!' said Judith eagerly, flinging herself against him and putting both arms round his neck confidingly—'Lo, I trust thee more than any man! Lead me from hence; we will move slowly and with care,—thou shalt hold me near thy heart,—the path is straight adown the hill,—the crosses of the criminals are at the summit, as thou knowest, and if we trace the homeward track from here surely it will be easy to feel the way.'

'What of the multitude?' said Barabbas—'Thou knowest not, Judith, how wildly they are scattered, —how in their straying numbers they do obstruct the ground at every turn,—and it is as though one walked at the bottom of the sea at midnight, without the shine of moon or stars.'

'Nevertheless, if thou lovest me, thou wilt lead me,'—repeated Judith imperatively. 'But thou dost not love me!'

'I do not love thee! I!' Barabbas paused,—then caught the twining arms from about his neck and held them hard. 'So well do I love thee, Judith, that, if thou playest me false, I can hate thee! 'Tis thou that art of dubious mind in love. I have loved only thee; but thou, perchance, since I was chained in prison, hast loved others. Is it not so? Speak!'

For all answer she clung about his neck again and began to weep complainingly.

'Ah, cruel Barabbas!' she wailed to him between her sobs,—'Thou standest here in this darkness, prating of love while death doth threaten us. Lead me away, I tell thee, — take me homeward, — and thou shalt have thy reward. Thou wilt not move from this accursed place which hath been darkened and confused by the evil spells of the Nazarene,—thou

wilt let me perish here, because thou dost prize thine
own life more than mine!'

'Judith! Judith!' cried Barabbas in agony—'Thou
dost break my heart,—thou dost torture my soul!
Beware how thou speakest of the dying Prophet of
Galilee,—for thou didst taunt Him in His pain,—
and this darkness fell upon us when thy cruel words
were spoken! Come,—if thou must come; but remember there is neither sight nor sense nor order in
the scattered multitude through which we must fight
our passage,—'twere safer to remain here,—together,
—and pray.'

'I will not pray to God so long as He doth
wantonly afflict us!' cried Judith loudly and im-
periously—'Let Him strike slaves with fear,—I am
not one to be so commanded! An' thou wilt not
help me, I will help myself; I will stay no longer
here to be slain by the tempest, when with courage
I might reach a place of safety.'

She moved a step away,— Barabbas caught her
mantle.

'Be it as thou wilt!' he said, driven to desperation
by her words,—'Only let me hold thee thus,'—and

he placed one arm firmly round her,—'Now measure each pace heedfully,—walk warily lest thou stumble over some swooning human creature,—and with thy hands feel the air as thou goest, for there are many dangers.'

As he thus yielded to her persuasions, she nestled against him caressingly, and lifted her face to his. In the gloom their lips met, and Barabbas, thrilled through every pulse of his being by that voluntary kiss of love, forgot his doubts, his suspicions, his sorrows, his supernatural forebodings and fears, and moved on with her through the darkness as a lost and doomed lover might move with his soul's ruin through the black depths of hell.

XIX

SLOWLY and cautiously they groped their way
along, and for two or three yards met with no
obstacle. Judith was triumphant, and with every
advancing step she took, began to feel more and
more secure.

'Did I not tell thee how it would be?' she
said exultingly, as she clung close to Barabbas,—
'Danger flies from the brave-hearted, and ere we
know it, we shall find ourselves at the foot of the
hill.'

'And then'—murmured Barabbas dubiously.

'Then, doubt not but that we shall discover
light and guidance. And I will take thee to my
father's house, and tell him thou hast aided in my
rescue, and he will remember that thou hast been
freed from prison by the people's vote, and he

will overlook thy past, and receive thee with honour. Will that not satisfy thee and make thee proud?'

He shuddered and sighed heavily.

'Alas, Judith, honour and I are for ever parted, and I shall never be proud of aught in this world again! There is a sorrow on my heart too heavy for me to lift,—perchance 'tis my love for thee,—perchance 'tis the weight of mine own folly and wickedness; but be the burden what it may, I am stricken by a grief that will not vent itself in words. For 'tis I, Judith, I who should have died to-day, instead of the holy "Nazarene"!'

She gave an exclamation of contempt, and laughed.

'Callest thou him holy?' she cried derisively— 'Then thou art mad!—or thou hast a devil! A malefactor, a deceiver, a trickster, a blasphemer,—and holy!'

Another light laugh rippled from her lips, but was quickly muffled, for Barabbas laid his hands upon her mouth.

'Hush,—hush!' he muttered,—'Be pitiful. Some

one is weeping, . . . out there in the gloom!
Hush!'

She struggled with him angrily, and twisted herself
out of his hold.

'What do I care who weeps or laughs?' she exclaimed,—'Why dost thou pause? Art stricken
motionless?'

But Barabbas replied not. He was listening to a
melancholy sobbing sound that trembled through the
darkness,—the sorrowing clamour of a woman's
breaking heart,—and a strange anguish oppressed
him.

'Come!' cried Judith.

He roused himself with an effort.

'I can go no further with thee, Judith,'—he said
sadly,—'Something,—I know not what,—drags me
back. I am giddy,—faint,—I cannot move!'

'Coward!' she exclaimed—'Farewell then! I go
on without thee.'

She sprang forward—but he caught at her robe
and detained her.

'Nay,—have patience,—wait but a moment'—
he implored in tones that were hoarse and unsteady

—'I will force my steps on with thee, even if I die.
I have sinned for thy sake in the past—it matters
little if I sin again. But from my soul I do
beseech thee that thou say no more evil of the
"Nazarene"!'

'What art thou, that thou should'st so command
me?' she demanded contemptuously,—'And what
has the "Nazarene" to do with thee, save that he
was sentenced to death instead of thee? Thou
weak slave! Thou, who didst steal pearls only
because I said I loved such trinkets!—oh, worthy
Barabbas, to perjure thyself for a woman's whim!
—thou, who didst slay Gabrias because he loved
me!'

'Judith!' A sudden access of fury heated his
blood,—and seizing her in both arms roughly he held
her as in a vice. 'This is no time for folly,—and
whether this darkness be of heaven or hell, thou
darest not swear falsely with death so close about us!
Take heed of me! for if thou liest I will slay thee!
Callest thou me weak? Nay, I am strong,—strong
to love and strong to hate, and as evil in mind and
passion as any man! I will know the truth of

thee, Judith, before I `move, or let thee move another inch from hence! Gabrias loved thee, thou sayest, — come, confess! — didst thou, in thy turn, love Gabrias?'

She writhed herself to and fro in his grasp rebelliously.

'I love no man!' she cried in defiance and anger. 'All men love *me!* Am I not the fairest woman in Judæa?—and thou speakest to me of one lover—one! And thou would'st be that one thyself? O fool! What aileth thee? Lo, thou hast me here in thine arms,—thou canst take thy fill of kisses an' thou wilt,—I care naught, so long as thou dost not linger on this midnight way. I offer thee my lips,—I am thy sole companion for a little space,—be grateful and content that thou hast so much. Gabrias loved me, I tell thee,—with passion, yet guardedly,—but now there are many greater than he who love me, and who have not his skill to hide their thought'——

'Such as the high-priest Caiaphas!' interrupted Barabbas in choked, fierce accents.

She gave a little low laugh of triumph and malice commingled.

'Come!' she said, disdaining to refute his suggestion,—'Come, and trouble not thyself concerning
others, when for this hour at least I am all thine.
Rejoice in the advantage this darkness gives thee,—
lo, I repel thee not!—only come, and waste no more
precious time in foolish questioning.'

He loosened his arms abruptly from about her, and
stood motionless.

'Come!' she cried again.

He gave her no response.

She rushed at him and clutched him by his mantle,
putting up her soft face to his, and showering light
kisses on his lips and throat.

'Barabbas, come!' she clamoured in his ears—
'Lead me onward!—thou shalt have love enough for
many days!'

He thrust her away from him loathingly.

'Get thee hence!' he cried,—'Fairest woman of
Judæa, as thou callest thyself and as thou art, tempt
me no more, lest in these hellish vapours I murder
thee! Yea, even as I murdered Gabrias! Had
I thought his boast of thee was true, *he* should have
lived, and *thou* should'st have been slain! Get thee

hence, thou ruin of men!—get thee hence,—alone!
I will not go with thee!—I tear the love of thee from
out my heart, and if I ever suffer thy fair false face
to haunt my memory, may Heaven curse my soul!
I take shame upon myself that I did ever love thee,
thou evil snare!—deceive others as thou wilt, thou
shalt deceive Barabbas no more!'

Again she laughed, a silvery mocking laugh, and
like some soft lithe snake, twined herself fawningly
about him.

'No more?' she queried in dulcet whispers—'Thou
wilt not be deceived, thou poor Barabbas?—thou wilt
not be caressed?—thou wilt no longer be my slave?
Alas, thou canst not help thyself, good fool!—I feel
thee tremble,—I hear thee sigh!—come,—come!'
and she pulled him persuasively by the arm,—'Come!
—and perchance thou shalt have a victory thou
dreamest not of!'

For one dizzy moment he half yielded, and suffered
himself to be dragged forward a few paces like a man
in a dull stupor of fever or delirium,—then, the overpowering emotion he had felt before came upon him
with tenfold force, and again he stopped.

'No!' he exclaimed—'No, I will not! I cannot! No more, no more! I will go no further!'

'Die then, fool, in thy folly!' she cried, and bounded away from him into the gloom. Hardly had she disappeared, when a monster clap of thunder burst the sky, and a ball of fire fell to earth, hissing its way through the darkness like a breaking bomb. At the same instant, with subterranean swirl and rumble the ground yawned asunder in a wide chasm, from which arose serpentine twists of fiery vapour and forked tongues of flame. Paralysed with horror, Barabbas stared distractedly at this terrific phenomenon, and as he looked, saw the lately vanished Judith made suddenly visible in a glory of volcanic splendour. Her figure, brilliantly lighted up by the fierce red glow, was on the very edge of the hideous chasm, and appeared to blaze there like a spirit of fire. Had she gone one step further, she would have been engulfed within its depths,—as it was she had escaped by a miracle. For one moment Barabbas beheld her thus, a glittering phantom as she seemed, surrounded by dense pyramids of smoke and jets of flame,—then, with another underground roar and trembling the ghastly light was quenched, and blackness closed in again, — impenetrable blackness, in which nothing could be seen, and nothing heard, save the shrieks and groans of the people.

XX

THE panic was now universal and uncontrollable. Crowds of frantic creatures, struggling, scream-ing, weeping, and fighting invisibly with one another, rushed madly up and down in the darkness, flinging themselves forward and backward like the swirling waves of a sea. The murky air resounded with yells and curses,—now and then a peal of hideous laughter rang out, and sometimes a piercing scream of pain or terror, while under all these louder and more desperate noises ran the monotonous murmuring of prayer. The impression and expectation of renewed disaster burdened the minds of all ; the shuddering trouble of the earth had terrified the boldest, and many were in momentary dread that the whole hill of Calvary would crumble beneath them and swallow them up in an abyss of fire. Barabbas stood still where Judith had left him,—his limbs quivering, and a cold sweat breaking out over all his body,—yet he was not so much conscious of fear as of horror,—horror and shame of himself and of the whole world. An ineffaceable guilt seemed branded on mankind,—though how this conviction was borne in upon him he could not tell. Presently, determining to move, he began to retrace his steps cautiously backward, wondering, with a sinking heart, whether Judith had still gone on. She must have realised her danger; she would never have proceeded further, knowing of that frightful rent in the ground, into which, in her wilful recklessness, she had so nearly plunged. Once he called 'Judith!' loudly, but there was no response.

Stumbling along in doubt and dread, his foot suddenly came in contact with a figure lying prone, and stooping to trace its outline, he touched cold steel.

'Take heed, whosoe'er thou art,' said a smothered voice, 'and wound not thyself against my sword-edge. I am Petronius.'

'Dost thou find safety here, soldier?' inquired

Barabbas tremulously—'Knowest thou where thou art in this darkness?'

'I have not moved from hence'—replied Petronius; 'I was struck as by a shock from heaven, and I have stayed as I fell. What would it avail me to wander up and down? Moreover, such as I am, die at their post, if die they must,—and my post is here, close by the Cross of the "Nazarene."'

Barabbas shuddered, and his blood grew cold in his veins.

'Is He dead?' he asked in hushed awed accents.

'Nay, He breathes yet'—replied the centurion with equal emotion,—'And,—He suffers!'

Yielding to an overwhelming impulse of passion and pain, Barabbas groped his way on a few steps, and then, halting, stretched out his hands.

'Where art Thou?' he muttered faintly —'O Thou who diest in my wretched stead, where art Thou?'

He listened, but caught no sound save that of sobbing.

Keeping his hands extended, he felt the dense air up and down.

'Who is it that weeps?' he asked, softening his voice to its gentlest tone—'Speak to me, I beseech thee!—whether man or woman, speak! for behold I am a sinner and sorrowful as thou!'

A long, low gasping sigh quivered through the gloom,—a sigh of patient pain; and Barabbas, knowing instinctively Who it was that thus expressed His human sense of torture, was seized by an agony he could not quell.

'Where art thou?' he implored again in indescribable anxiety—'I cannot feel thee,—I cannot find thee! Darkness covers the world and I am lost within it! Thy sufferings, Nazarene, exceed all speech, yet, evil man as I am, I swear my heart is ready to break with thine!'

And as he thus spoke involuntarily and incoherently, he flung himself on his knees, and scalding tears rushed to his eyes. A trembling hand touched him,—a woman's hand.

'Hush!' whispered a broken voice in the gloom—'Thou poor, self-tormented sinner, calm thyself, and pray! Fear not; count not up thy transgressions, for were they more numerous than the grains of sand in the desert, thy tears and sorrows here should win thy pardon. Kneel with us, if thou wilt, and watch; for the end approaches,—the shadows are passing, and light is near.'

' If this be so,' said Barabbas, gently detaining the small hand that touched him—' Why dost thou still continue to weep? Who art thou that art so prodigal of tears?'

' Naught but woman,'—answered the sweet whispering voice—'And as woman I weep,—for the great Love's wrong!'

She withdrew her hand from his clasp,—and he remained where he was beside her, quietly kneeling. Conscious of the nearness of the Cross of the ' Nazarene' and of those who were grouped about it, he felt no longer alone,—but the weight of the mysterious sorrow he carried within himself perceptibly increased. It oppressed his heart and bewildered his brain,—the darkness seemed to encircle him with an almost palpable density,—and he began to consider vaguely that it would be well for him, if he too might die on Calvary with that mystic ' King' whose personality had exercised so

great a fascination over him. What had he to live
for? Nothing. He was outcast through his own
wickedness, and as the memory of his sins clouded his
mind he grew appalled at the evil in his own nature.
His crimes of theft and murder were the results of his
blind passion for Judith Iscariot,—and this blind
passion now seemed to him the worst crime of all.
For this his name and honour were gone,—for this
he had become a monster of iniquity in his own sight.
Yet,—strange to say, only that very morning, he had
not thought himself so vile. Between the hours of
his being brought before Pilate, and now,—when he
knelt in this supernatural darkness before the unseen
dying 'Man of Nazareth,' an age seemed to have
passed,—a cycle of time burdened with histories,—
histories of the soul and secret conscience, which are
of more weight in God's countings than the histories
of empires. The people had released him,—they had
hailed him, the liberated thief and murderer, with
acclamations,—true!—but what was all this popular
clamour worth, when in his own heart he knew himself to be guilty of the utmost worst that could be
done to him? Oh, the horrible, horrible burden of

recognised sin!—the dragging leaden weight that ties the immortal spirit down to grossness and materialism, when it would fain wing its way to the highest attainment!—the crushing consciousness of being driven back into darkness out of light supernal! of being thrust away, as it were, with loathing, out of the sight and knowledge of the Divine! This was a part of the anguish of Barabbas,—a mental anguish he had never felt till now,—and this was why he almost envied his former comrade Hanan for having been elected to die in the companionship of the 'Nazarene.' All these thoughts of his were purely instinctive; he could not reason out his emotions, because they were unlike himself and new to him. Nevertheless, if he uttered a prayer at all while kneeling in that solemn gloom, it was for death, not life.

And now, all suddenly through the heavy murk, a muffled clangour stirred the air,—the tolling of great bells and smaller chimes from the city. Swinging and jangling, they made themselves heard distinctly for the first time since the darkness fell over the land,—a sign that the atmosphere was growing clearer.

They were ringing out the hour of sunset, though no sun was visible. And, as they rang, Barabbas felt that some one near him moved softly among the shadows, and stood upright. He strove to discern the outline of that risen shape, and presently, to his intense amazement, saw a pale light begin to radiate through the vapours and gradually weave a faintly luminous halo round the majestic form of a Woman, whose face, divinely beautiful, supremely sad, shone forth from the darkness like a star, and whose clasped hands were stretched towards the great invisible Cross in an attitude of yearning and prayer. And the bells rang and the light widened, and in two or three moments more, a jagged rift of dusky red opened in the black sky. Broadening slowly, it spread a crimson circle in the heavens immediately behind the summit of the Cross of the 'Nazarene;'—first casting ruddy flashes on the inscribed letters, 'Jesus of Nazareth, King of the Jews,' and then illumining with a flame-like glow the grand thorn-crowned head of the Crucified. Ah, what sublime, unspeakable, mystic agony was written now upon that face Divine! Horror of the world's sin,—pity for the world's woe,—love for the

world's poor creatures, — and the passionate God's
yearning for the world's pardon and better hope of
heaven,—all these great selfless thoughts were seen
in the indescribably beautiful expression of the pallid
features, the upward straining eyes,—the quivering,
tender lips ;—and Barabbas, staring at the wondrous
sight, felt as though his very soul and body must melt
and be dissolved in tears for such a kingly Sorrow !
The blood-red cleft in the sky lengthened,— and,
presently, shooting forth arrowy beams as of fire,
showed a strange and solemn spectacle. For as far
as eye could see in the lurid storm-light, the whole
multitude of the people upon Calvary were discovered
kneeling before the Cross of Christ ! All faces were
turned towards the dying Saviour ; in trouble, in fear
and desperation, every human creature there had
fallen unknowingly before their only Rescue whose
name was Love !—and, as the darkness broke up and
parted in long wavy lines, the widening radiance of
the heavens revealed what seemed to be a worshipping
world ! . . . But only for an instant, — for with the
gathering, growing light, came the rush of every-day
life and movement,—the prostrate crowd leaped up

with shouts of joy, glad exclamations of relief and laughter,—danger was over,—death no longer seemed imminent,—and as a natural result, God was forgotten. The thunder still growled heavily, but its echoes were rolling off into the far distance. And while the people grew more and more animated, scattering themselves in every direction, finding and embracing their friends and narrating their past fears, Barabbas rose also from his knees, wondering, awed and afraid. Directly facing him was the Cross of the ' Nazarene,' —but, beside him was—the Magdalen ! With her he had knelt in the deep darkness,—it must have been her hand that had touched him,—it must have been her voice that had so gently soothed him. He trembled ; she was a woman of many sins,—yet was she — was she so much worse than — than Judith ? His soul sickened as this comparison crossed his mind; yet, loathe it as he might, it still forced itself upon his attention. Judith Iscariot, beautiful, imperious, and triumphant in the secrecy of undiscovered sin, — Mary Magdalene, beautiful also, but broken-hearted, humbled to the dust of contempt, openly shamed, — and — penitent.

Which of the twain deserved the greater con-
demnation?

A deep sigh broke from his lips,—a sigh that was
almost a groan; an evil man himself, what right had
he to judge of evil women! Just then the Magdalen
raised her tear-wet eyes and looked at him,—her
luxuriant hair fell about her like a golden veil,—her
mouth quivered as though she were about to speak,
—but as she met his sternly meditative gaze, she
recoiled, and hiding her face in the folds of her mantle,
dragged herself nearer to the foot of the Cross, and
crouched there, motionless. And the other woman,—
she for whom, as Barabbas imagined, the welcome
light had been kindled in the beginning,—what of
her? She no longer stood erect as when the bells
had rung,—she had fallen once more upon her knees,
and her face, too, was hidden.

Suddenly a voice, pulsating with keenest anguish,
yet sweet and resonant, pealed through the air:

'*Eli, Eli, lama sabacthani!*'

With one accord the moving populace all came to
an abrupt halt, and every eye was turned towards the
central Cross from whence these thrilling accents

rang. Bars of gold were in the sky,—and now, the long-vanished sun, red as a world on fire, showed itself in round splendour above the summit of Calvary.

'*Eli, Eli, lama sabacthani!*' cried the rich agonised voice again, and the penetrating appeal, piercing aloft, was caught up in the breaking clouds and lost in answering thunder.

'*He calleth for Elias!*' exclaimed a man, one of those in the front rank of the crowd that was now pressing itself towards the Cross in morbid curiosity, —'*Let us see whether Elias will come to take him down!*'

And he laughed derisively.

Meanwhile Petronius, the centurion, looked up,— and saw that the last great agony of death was on the 'Nazarene.' Death in the bloom of life,—death, when every strong human nerve and sinew and drop of blood most potently rebelled at such premature dissolution,—death in a torture more hideous than imagination can depict or speech describe,—this was the fate that now darkly descended upon divinest Purity, divinest Love! Terrible shudderings ran

through the firm, heroically moulded Man's frame,—
the beautiful eyes were rolled up and fixed,—the lips
were parted, and the struggling breath panted forth
in short quick gasps. The fiery gold radiance of the
heavens spread itself out in wider glory,—the sun was
sinking rapidly. Moved by an impulse of compassion,
Petronius whispered to a soldier standing by, who,
obeying his officer's suggestion, dipped a sponge in
vinegar and placing it on a tall reed, lifted it to the
lips of the immortal Sufferer,' with the intention of
moistening the parched tongue and reviving the
swooning senses. But there was no sign that He was
conscious,—and while the soldier still endeavoured to
pass the sponge gently over the bleeding brows to
cool and comfort the torn and aching flesh, the sleek
priest Annas stepped forward from amongst the
people and interfered.

'*Let be,—let be!*' said he suavely, and with a meek
smile,—'*Let us see whether Elias will come to save
him!*'

The crowd murmured approval, — the soldier
dropped the reed, and glancing at Petronius, drew
back and stood apart. Petronius frowned heavily,

and surveyed the portly priest with all a martial
Roman's anger and disdain ; then he raised his eyes
again, sorrowfully and remorsefully, to the tortured
figure of the Crucified. Harder and faster came the
panting breath ; and, by some inexplicable instinct all
the soldiers and as many of the multitude as could
get near, gathered together in solemn silence, and
stared up as though fascinated by some mystic spell,
at the last fierce struggle between that pure Body and
divine Spirit. The sun was disappearing,—and from
its falling disc, huge beams rose up on every side,
driving all the black and thunderous clouds in the
direction of Jerusalem, where they hung darkening
over the city and Solomon's Temple. Suddenly the
difficult breathing of the 'Nazarene' ceased; a
marvellous luminance fell on the upturned face,—the
lips that had been parted in gasping agony closed
in a dreamy smile of perfect peace,—and a flaming
golden glory, wing-shaped and splendid, woven as it
seemed out of all the varying hues of both storm and
sunset, spread itself on either side of the Cross.
Upward, to the topmost visible height of heaven these
giant cloud-pinions towered plume-wise, and between

them, and behind the dying Christ, the sun, now sunk
to a half-circle, glittered like an enormous jewelled
monstrance for the Host in some cathedral of air.
In the midst of this ethereal radiance the pale face of
the world's Redeemer shone forth, rapt and transfigured
by mysterious ecstasy,—and His voice, faint, solemn,
but melodious as music itself, thrilled softly through
the light and silence :

'Father! Into Thy hands ... I commend—My Spirit!'

As the words were uttered, Petronius and the soldier
who had proffered the vinegar, exchanged a glance,—
a rapid glance of mutual suggestion and understanding. With assumed roughness and impatience,
the soldier raised his spear and deliberately thrust it
deep into the side of the dying ' Nazarene.' A stream
of blood gushed out, mingled with water ; and the man
whose merciful desire to put an end to torture had
thus impelled him to pierce the delicate flesh, sprang
back, vaguely affrighted at what he had done. For,
with the sharp shock of the blow, the thorn-crowned
Head drooped suddenly,—the eyes that had been
turned to heaven now looked down, . . . down, for
the last time to earth, . . . and rested upon the

watching crowd with such an unspeakable passion of
pity, love and yearning, that all the people were
silent, stricken with something like shame as well as
awe.   Never again in all the centuries to come would
such a Love look down upon Humanity!—never again
would the erring world receive such a sublime Forgiveness!—such a tender parting Benediction!   The
wondrous smile still lingered on the pale lips,—a light
more glorious than all the sunshine that ever fell on
earth illumined the divinely beautiful features.   One
last, lingering, compassionate gaze,—the clear, searching, consciously supernal gaze of an immortal God
bidding farewell for ever to mortality, and then, . . .
with an exulting sweetness and solemnity, the final
words were uttered :

  ' *It is finished!* '

The fair head fell forward heavily on the chest,—
the tortured limbs quivered once . . . twice . . . and
then were still!   Death had apparently claimed its
own,—and no sign was given to show that Death itself
was mastered.   All was over ;—God's Message had
been given, and God's Messenger slain.   The law was
satisfied with its own justice !   A god could not have

died, — but He who had been called the 'Son of God' was dead! It was 'finished;' — the winged glory in the skies folded itself up and fled away; and like a torch inverted, the red sun dropped into the night.

XXI

A BRIEF pause ensued. The solemn hush that even in a callous crowd invariably attends the actual presence of death reigned unbroken for a while, —then one man moved, another spoke, the spell of silence gave way to noise and general activity, and the people began to disperse hastily, eager to get back safely to their homes before the deepening night entirely closed in. Some compassion was expressed for the women who were crouched at the foot of the 'Nazarene's' Cross,—but no one went near them, or endeavoured to rouse them from their forlorn attitudes. Barabbas had, unconsciously to himself, recoiled from the horror of beholding the Divine death-agony, and now stood apart, his eyes fixed on the ground and his tired body quivering in every limb. The populace appeared to have forgotten him,—they drifted past him in shoals, talking, laughing, and seemingly no longer seriously oppressed by the recollection of the terrifying events of the afternoon. The three crosses stood out black against the darkening sky;—the executioners were beginning to take down the body of Hanan, in which a few wretched gasps of life still lingered. Looking from right to left, Barabbas could see no face familiar to him,—the high-priests Caiaphas and Annas had disappeared,—there was no sign of Judith Iscariot anywhere, and he could not even perceive the striking and quaintly garbed figure of his mysterious acquaintance Melchior. The only person he recognised was Petronius the centurion, who was still at his post by the central Cross, and who by his passive attitude and downcast eyes appeared to be absorbed in melancholy meditation. Barabbas approached him, and saw that his rough bearded face was wet with tears.

'*Truly*,' he muttered beneath his breath as he thrust his sword of office back into its scabbard—'*Truly this Man was the Son of God!*'

Barabbas caught the words, and stared at him in questioning terror.

'Thinkest thou so?' he faltered—'Then . . . what shall be done to those who have slain Him?'

'I know not,'—answered Petronius,—'I am an ignorant fool. But perchance no more ignorant than they who did prefer thy life, Barabbas, to the life of the "Nazarene." Nay, look not so heavily!—thou art not to blame,—'twas not thy choosing. 'Twas not even the people's choosing—'twas the priests' will! A curse on priests, say I!—they have worked all the evil in the world from the beginning, blaspheming the names of the Divine to serve their ends. This Crucified Man was against priestcraft,—hence His doom. But I tell thee this same "King of the Jews," as they called Him, was diviner than any of the gods I wot of,—and mark me!—we have not seen or heard the last of Him!'

He turned away with a kind of fierce impatience and shame of his own emotion, and resumed his duty, that of superintending the taking down of the three crucified bodies from their respective trees of torture. Barabbas sighed, and stood looking on, pained and irresolute. The shadows of night darkened swiftly,— and the figure of the dead Christ above him seemed

strange and spectral,—pathetic in its helplessness,—
yet . . . after all,—a beautiful lifeless body,—and . . .
nothing more! A sense of bitter disappointment
stole over him. He now realised that throughout
the whole of the terrible tragedy, he had, unconsciously to himself, believed it impossible for the
wondrous 'Man of Nazareth' to die. The impression
had been firmly fixed in his mind, he knew not how,
that at the last moment, some miracle would be
enacted in the presence of the whole multitude;—
that either the Cross itself would refuse to hold its
burden,—or that some divinely potent messenger
from heaven, whose heralds had been the storm
and earthquake, would suddenly descend in glory
and proclaim the suffering 'Prophet' as the true
Messiah. Surely if He had been indeed the 'Son
of God,' as Petronius said, His power would have
been thus declared! To Barabbas the present end
of things seemed inadequate. Death was the ordinary fate of men; he would have had the kingly
'Nazarene' escape the common lot. And while he
pondered the bewildering problem, half in vexation,
half in sorrow, a voice said softly in his ear,—

'*It is finished !*'

He started, and turned to behold his friend, the mystic Melchior, whose dark features were ghastly with a great pallor, but who nevertheless forced a grave and kindly smile as he repeated,—

'*It is finished!* Didst thou not also, with all the rest of the world, receive that marvellous assurance? Henceforth there will be no true man alive who fears to die! Come; we have no more to do here;—our presence is somewhat of a sacrilege. Leave the dead Christ to the tears and lamentations of the women who loved Him. We men have done our part; we have murdered Him!'

He drew Barabbas away, despite his expressed reluctance.

'I tell thee,' he said—'thou shalt see this Wonder of the Ages again at an hour thou dreamest not of. Meantime, come with me, and hesitate no more to follow out thy destiny.'

'My destiny!' echoed Barabbas—'Stranger, thou dost mock me! If thou hast any mystic power, read my soul, and measure its misery. I have no destiny save despair.'

'Despair is a blank prospect'—said his companion tranquilly, 'Nevertheless because a woman is false and thy soul is weak, thou needest not at once make bosom-friends with desperation. Didst thou discover thy Judith in the darkness?'

The sombre eyes of Barabbas flashed with mingled wrath and anguish as he answered,

'Ay,—I found her,—and,—I lost her!'

'Never was loss so fraught with gain!'—said Melchior—'I saw her, when the light began to pierce the storm-clouds, hurrying swiftly down the hill citywards.'

'Then she is safe!' exclaimed Barabbas, unable to conceal the joy he felt at this news.

'Truly she is, — or she should be,' responded Melchior; 'She had most excellent saintly protection. The high-priest Caiaphas was with her.'

Barabbas uttered a fierce oath and clenched his fist. Melchior observed him attentively.

'Methinks thou art still in her toils,' he said—'Untutored savage as thou art, thou canst not master thy ruffian passions. Nevertheless I will yet have patience with thee.'

' *Thou* wilt have patience with me!' muttered
Barabbas with irritation,—' *Thou* wilt! Nay, but
who art thou, and what hast thou to do with me,
now or at any future time?'

' What have I to do with thee?' repeated Melchior
—' Why—nothing! Only this. That being studi-
ously inclined, I make thee an object of my study.
Thou art an emblem of thy race in days to come,
Barabbas;—as I before told thee, thou art as much
the symbol of the Israelites as yonder crucified
" Nazarene" is the symbol of a new faith and civilisa-
tion. Did I not say to thee a while ago that
thou, and not He, must be from henceforth " King
of the Jews"?'

' I understand thee not,' said Barabbas wearily—
' Thou wilt ever speak in parables!'

' 'Tis the custom of the East '—answered Melchior
composedly,—' And I will read thee the parable of
thyself at some more fitting time. At present the
night is close upon us, and there is yet much to be
done for the world's wonderment, . . . stay!—whom
have we here?'

He stopped abruptly, holding Barabbas back by

the arm. They had nearly stumbled over the prostrate form of a man who was stretched out on the turf, face downward, giving no other sign of life save a convulsive clutching movement of his hands. Melchior bent over him and tried to raise him, but his limbs were so rigidly extended that he appeared to be positively nailed to the ground.

'He is in some fit, or hath the falling-sickness '— said Barabbas,—'Or he hath been smitten thus with terror of the earthquake.'

All at once, as they still made efforts to lift him, the fallen man turned up a ghastly face and stared at them, as though he saw some hideous and appalling vision. Tearing up handfuls of the grass and earth in his restless fingers, he struggled into a kneeling posture, and still surveyed them with so much wildness and ferocity that they involuntarily drew back, amazed.

'What will ye do to me?' he muttered hoarsely,— 'What death will ye contrive? Stretch me on a rack of burning iron,—tear my bones one by one from out my flesh,—let the poisoned false blood ooze out drop by drop from my veins,—do all this and ye shall not punish me as I deserve! There are no ways of torture left for such an one as I am!' And with a frightful cry he suddenly leaped erect. 'Coward,' coward, coward!' he shrieked, tossing his arms wildly in the air. 'Coward! Brand it on the face of heaven!—the only name left to me—coward! False, treacherous coward! Write it on stone,—post it up in every city,—shout it in the streets—tell all the world of me,—me, the wretched and accursed man,—the follower of the Christ,—the faithless servant who denied his Master!'

With another terrible cry, he again flung himself on the ground, and throwing his arms over his head, wept aloud in all the fierce abandonment of a strong man's utter misery.

Melchior and Barabbas stood beside him, silent. At last Melchior spoke.

'If thou art Peter'—he began.

'Oh, that I were not!' cried the unhappy man—'Oh, that I were anything in the world,—a dog, a stone, a clod of earth,—anything but myself! Look you, what is a man worth, who, in the hour of trial, deserts his friend? And such a Friend!—a

King — a God!' Tears choked his voice for a moment's space; then raising his forlorn head, he looked piteously at his interlocutors. 'Ye are strangers to me'—he said—'Why do ye stand there pitying? Ye know naught of what has chanced concerning the Man of Nazareth.'

'We know all,' — replied Melchior with grave gentleness—'And for the "Nazarene," grieve not, inasmuch as His sorrows are over,—He is dead.'

'Ye know naught—naught of the truth!' cried Peter despairingly—'That He is dead is manifest, for the world is dark as hell without Him! Yea, He is dead;—but ye know not how His death was wrought! I watched Him die;—afar off I stood,—always afar off!—afraid to approach Him,—afraid to seek His pardon,—afraid of His goodness,—afraid of my wickedness. Last night He looked at me,—looked at me straightly when I spoke a lie. Three times did I falsely swear I never knew Him,—and He,—He said no word, but only looked and gently smiled. Why, oh, why'—moaned the miserable man, breaking into tears again,—'why, when I denied His friendship did He not slay me?—why did not the earth then open and swallow me in fire! Nay, there was no quick vengeance taken,—only that one look of His,—that look of pity and of love!—O God, O God! I feel those heavenly Eyes upon me now, searching the secrets of my soul!'

Weeping, he hid his face,—his wretchedness was so complete and crushing that the hardest and most unpitying heart in the world would have been moved to compassion for such bitter and remorseful agony. Barabbas, inclined to despise him at first for the confession of his base cowardice, relented somewhat at the sight of so much desperation, and there was a certain touch of tenderness in the austerity of Melchior's manner, as with a few earnest words he persuaded the sorrowing disciple to rise and lean upon his arm.

'What is past is past,'—he said gravely—'Thou canst never undo, Peter, what thou hast done,—and this falsehood of thine must needs be chronicled for all time as a token to prove a truth,—the awful truth that often by one act, one word, man makes his destiny. Alas for thee, Peter, that thou too must serve as symbol! A symbol of error,—for on thy one lie, self-serving men will build a fabric of lies in which the Master whom thou hast denied will have no part. I know thy remorse is great as thy sin, — yet not even remorse can change the law, — for every deed, good or evil, that is done in this world, works out its own inexorable result. Nevertheless thou hast not erred so wickedly as thy fellow, Judas.'

'Nay, but he could die!' cried Peter, turning his wild white face to the dark heavens — 'Judas could die! — but I, coward as I am, live on!'

Barabbas started violently.

'Die!' he exclaimed, 'What sayest thou? Judas? Judas Iscariot? — He is not dead?'

Peter threw up his arms with a frenzied gesture of despair.

'Not dead? — not dead?' — he echoed shrilly — 'If ye do not believe me, come and see! Come! Down by Gethsemane ye will find him, — outside the garden, in a dark hollow sloping downward like a grave, — under the thickest shadows of the olive-trees, and close to the spot where he betrayed the Master.

There ye shall behold him!' and his agonised voice
sank to a shuddering whisper; 'His body hangs
from a gnarled leafless branch like some untimely
fruit of hell,—some monstrous birth of devils!—
the very air seems poisoned by his livid corpse!
Horrible! . . . horrible! . . . ye know not how he
looks, . . . dead, . . . and swinging from the leafless bough! He slew himself thus last night rather
than face this day,—would to God I had done
likewise'!—so should I have been even as he, cold,
stiff, and free from torturing memory these many
hours!'

Overwhelmed by this new and unexpected horror,
Barabbas felt as though the earth were giving way
beneath him,—he staggered, and would have fallen
had not Melchior caught him by the arm.

'Judith!' he gasped hoarsely—'Judith!—her
brother—dead—and self-slain! How will she
bear it! Oh, my God, my God! who will tell
her!'

Peter heard the muttered words, and gave vent to
a bitter cry of misery and fury.

'Who will tell her!' he shrieked—'I will! I will

confront the fiend in woman's shape,—the mocking, smiling, sweet-voiced, damnëd devil who lured us on to treachery! Judith, sayest thou? Bring me to her,—confront me with her, and I will blazon forth the truth! I will rend heaven asunder with mine accusation!'

He shook his clenched hands aloft, and for the moment his grief-stricken face took upon itself a grandeur and sublimity of wrath that was almost superhuman.

'Who will tell her?' he repeated—'Not only I, but the slain Judas himself will tell her!—his fixed and glassy eyes will brand their curse upon her,—his stark dead body will lay its weight upon her life,—his dumb mouth will utter speechless oracles of vengeance! Accursed be her name for ever!—she knew,—she knew—how weak men are,—how blind, how mad, how fooled and frenzied by a woman's beauty,—she traded on her brother's tenderness, and with the witchery of her tongue she did beguile even me! Do I excuse mine own great wickedness?—Nay, for my fault was not of her persuasion, and I am in my own sight viler than any sinner that breathes,—but I say

she knew, as evil women all do know, the miserable
weakness of mankind, and knowing it, she had no
mercy! 'Tis she hath brought her brother to his
death,—for 'twas her subtle seeming-true persuasion that did work upon his mind and lead him
to betray the Master! Yea, 'twas even thus!—and
I will tell her so!—I will not shrink!—God
grant that every word I speak may be as a
dagger in her false, false heart to stab and torture
her for ever!'

His features were transfigured by strange fervour,
—a solemn passion, austere and menacing, glowed
in his anguished eyes, and Barabbas, with a wild
gesture of entreaty cried aloud,

'Man, undo thy curse! She is but a woman—and
—I loved her!'

Peter looked at him with a distracted, dreary smile.

'Loved her! Who art thou that speakest of
love in these days of death? Lo you, there is no
love left in all the world,—'tis crucified! Loved
her, thou sayest? Then come and see her work,
—come!—'tis a brave testimony of true love!—
come!'

He beckoned them mysteriously, and began to run before them. . . . Melchior stopped him.

'Where dost thou hasten, Peter?' he said gently. 'Thou art distraught with sorrow,—whither would'st thou have us follow thee?'

'To Gethsemane!' replied Peter, with a terrible look—'To Gethsemane,—but not inside the garden! No—no!—for there He, the Elect of God, the Messenger of Heaven, last night prayed alone,—and we, we His disciples, did we pray also? Nay—we slept!' and he broke into a discordant peal of delirious laughter—'We, being men, could find naught better to do than sleep! More senseless than the clods of earth on which we lay, we slumbered heavily inert, dead to our Master's presence, deaf to His voice! "Could ye not watch," said He, with soft patience to us, "with Me one hour?" No, not one hour!—it was not in us to forget ourselves in His grief, even for that space of time. We craved for sleep, and took it,— we could not sacrifice an hour's comfort for His sake! Why, all heaven was wakeful!—the very leaves and blades of grass must have found eyes to watch with Him,—we,—we men only, His friends and followers—

slept! Oh, 'twas brave of us!—'twas passing tender!
Mark ye thus the value of earth's love! we swore we
loved Him,—nevertheless we left Him. When the
guards came suddenly upon us, we all forsook Him
and fled,—I only followed Him, but afar off,—always
afar off! This is what man calls faithfulness!' He
paused, trembling violently, then resumed in impatience and agitation—'Come! not inside Gethsemane, for methinks there are angels there,—but
outside, where Judas waits! He is patient enough
now,—he will not move from thence till he is carried,
—will ye bear him home? Home to his father's
house!—lay him down at his sister's feet, while his
dead eyes stare beyond all life and time out to interminable doom!—Carry him home and lay him down!
—down before her who did wickedly and wantonly
work his ruin,—and let her weep—weep till tears
drown every vestige of her beauty, and yet she shall
never blot from her accursed life the memory of the
evil she hath done!'

'Oh, thou unpitying soul!' cried Barabbas desperately — 'What proof hast thou, thou self-
convicted false disciple, of Judith's wrong-doing?

How hath she merited thy malediction? Thou dost rave!—thy words are wild and without reason!— as coward thou didst deny thy Master,—as coward still thou wilt shift blame upon a woman! How canst thou judge of her, being thyself admittedly so vile?'

Peter looked at him in haggard misery.

'Vile truly am I'—he said—'And coward I have proclaimed myself. But who art thou? If I mistake not, thou art the people's chosen rescued prisoner,— Barabbas is thy name. Wert thou not thief and murderer? Art thou not vile? Art thou not coward? I reproach thee not for thy sins! Nevertheless I know who roused the baser part of me,—for every man hath a baser part,—and who did change the faithful Judas to a traitor. 'Twas subtly done,— 'twas even wise in seeming,—so cunningly contrived as to appear most truly for the best. Would ye know how? Then follow me as I bid—and I will tell all while my heart is full, for if God be merciful to me I shall not live long; and I must speak the truth before I die.'

He was calmer now and his words were more

coherent ; Melchior exchanged a meaning look with Barabbas, and they both silently prepared to follow him. As they began to walk forward slowly, a man, tall, and of singularly stately bearing, brushed past them in the darkness, and with a murmured word of apology and salutation pressed on in evident haste. Peter stopped abruptly, looking after him.

'Yonder goes Joseph of Arimathea'—he murmured, straining his eyes through the evening shadows to watch the swiftly receding figure—'A good man and a just. In secret he also was one of the Master's followers. Whither, I wonder, doth he bend his steps so late?'

He seemed troubled and perplexed ;—Melchior touched his arm to recall his wandering thoughts. He started as from a dream, and looked round with a vague smile. At that moment the moon rose, and lifting up a silver rim above Calvary, illumined with sudden ghostly radiance the three crosses on the summit of the hill. They were empty. With haggard face and piteous eyes, Peter gazed upwards and realised that the body of his Lord was taken down from the Cross and no longer visible,—and, covering his face in a fold of his mantle, he turned away and walked on slowly, while his companions following him in pitying silence heard the sound of smothered bitter weeping.

XXII

AT the foot of the hill they stopped.
To the left a tuft of palm-trees towered, and
under their spreading fan-like leaves was a well of
clear water, with a rough stone bench beside it.
The stars were beginning to sparkle thickly in the
sky, and the climbing moon already lit the landscape
with almost the clearness of day.

Peter uncovered his pallid face and looked awfully
around him.

'Here,' he said in trembling accents,—'here the
Master sat three days agone. Here did He discourse of marvels,—of the end of this world and of
the glory of the world to come, and flashing upon
us His eyes full of strange light and fire, He said,
"*Heaven and earth shall pass away, but My words shall
not pass away!*" Here,—only three days agone!'

He sighed heavily, and moving feebly to the stone bench, sank down upon it, shuddering.

'Bear with me, sirs, a while'—he murmured faintly; 'There is a mist before my sight, and I must rest ere I can walk further. Would ye not think me stricken old?—yet I am young—younger by two years than He who died to-day. Yea, we were all in the prime of youth and strength, we who followed Him,—and we should by very ardour of our blood have had some courage,—yet were we as weak and cowardly as though we had been dotards in the depth of age!'

His two companions said nothing. Barabbas, preoccupied with thoughts too wretched for utterance, sat down wearily on the projecting edge of the well, and stared darkly into the still water where a few stars were glitteringly reflected; Melchior stood, leaning slightly against one of the tall slim palm-tree stems, his picturesque saffron-hued garments appearing white in the early brilliance of the moon, and his dark features sternly composed and attentive. To him Peter turned his restless, weary eyes.

'Thou art of Egypt surely?' he said—'Thou hast the manner born of the land where men do chronicle the histories of life and time?'

Melchior met his questioning gaze tranquilly.

'Trouble not thy mind concerning me, thou forlorn disciple of the God!' he answered—'Whence I come or whither I go is of no more purport than the tossing hither and thither of a grain of dust or sand. Henceforward let no man set value on himself, since the Divine hath condescended to be humiliated even unto death.'

Peter scrutinised him yet more closely.

'Wert thou also His disciple?' he asked.

'As well inquire of me whether I feel the warmth and see the glory of the sun!'—responded Melchior— 'Those of my race and calling have known of Him these thousand years and waited for His coming. Nevertheless, touching these mysteries they are not for thy nation, Peter, nor for thy time,—wherefore I pray thee, if thou desirest to have speech with us on any matter, let it be now, and concern not thy mind with the creed of one who is, and ever will be a stranger to Judæa.'

He spoke gravely, gently, but with an air that repelled inquisitiveness.

Peter still kept his eyes fixed musingly upon him, —then he gave vent to another troubled sigh.

'Be it as thou wilt!' he said—'Yet truly thou dost call to mind the tale I have been told of certain kings that came to worship the Lord at Bethlehem, the night that He was born. 'Twas a strange history! and often have I marvelled how they could have known the very day and hour, . . . moreover there were wise men from the East'—He broke off,—then added hurriedly — 'Wert thou perchance one of these?'

Melchior shook his head slightly, a faint serious smile on his lips.

'Howbeit,' went on Peter with melancholy emotion; 'if thou dost ever write of this day, I pray thee write truly. For methinks the Jews will coin lies to cleanse this day from out the annals of their history.'

''Tis thou should'st write, Peter'—said Melchior with a keen look,—'And in thy chronicle confess thine own great sin.'

'I am no scribe'—replied the disciple sorrowfully;

'I have never learned the skill of letters. But if
I ever wrote, thinkest thou I would omit confession
of my frailty? Nay!—I would blazon it in words
of fire!' He paused with a wild look, then resumed
more calmly—'Sir, this will never be. I am an
ignorant man, and have no learning save that which
He of Nazareth taught, and which I was ever the last
to comprehend. Therefore I say, report my story
faithfully—and if thou wilt be just, say this of the
dead Judas,—that out of vain-glorious pride and love
he did betray his Master,—yea, out of love was born
the sin,—love and not treachery!'

Barabbas turned from his dreary contemplation of
the deep well-water, and fixed his brooding black
eyes upon the speaker, — Melchior still maintained
his attitude of grave and serene attention.

'Judith was treacherous'—continued Peter—'but
not so Judas. Beautiful as he was and young, his
thoughts aspired to good,—his dreams were for the
purification of the world, the happiness of all mankind. He loved the Master,—ay, with a great and
passionate love exceeding all of ours,—and he believed
in His Divinity and worshipped Him. He willingly

resigned home, country and kindred to follow Him,
— and now, having sinned against Him, he hath
given his life as penalty. Can mortal man do more?
God knoweth!'

He stopped again,—his breath came in a short
gasping sigh.

'When we entered Jerusalem a week agone'—he
continued slowly,—'Judas had been long absent
from his father's house, and long estranged from his
one sister whom he loved. Ye know the manner of
our coming to the city?—how the multitude rushed
forth to meet and greet Jesus of Nazareth, and called
Him "King," shouting "Hosannas" and strewing
His path with flowers and branches of the palm?
One who watched the crowd pass by said unto me—
"Why do ye not check this folly? Think ye the
priests will tamely bear the entrance of this Galilean
Prophet as a king? Nay, verily they will slay him
as a traitor!" And when I told these words to
Judas, he smiled right joyously, saying, "What need
we care for priestly malice? Truly our Master is a
King!—the King of Heaven, the King of earth!—
and all the powers of hell itself shall not prevail

against Him !'' Seeing his faith and love were such,
I said no more, though truly my heart misgave me.'

His eyes dwelt on the ground with an unseeing
dreary pain.

'That night, that very night on which we entered
Jerusalem, Judas went forth to see his sister. Oft
had he spoken of her fairness,—of the wonder of
her beauty, which, he would swear, was gorgeous
as the radiance of roses in the sun. He meant to
bring her to the Master's feet,—to tell her of His
teachings, His miracles, His wondrous tenderness
and love for all that were in sickness or in sorrow.
Light-hearted as a boy, he left us on this errand,—
but when he returned to us again, he was no more
the same. Sitting apart from us gloomy and absorbed in thought, oft-times I saw him gazing at our
Lord with a strange grief and yearning in his eyes
as though he sought to pierce the depth of some
great mystery. The days went on, till two evenings
before we shared with our Master the supper of the
Passover. Then Judas came to me, and taking me
aside, unburdened all his secret mind.'

Here Peter newly smitten by remorse and despair

gave an eloquent gesture half of wrath, half of suffering.

'Heaven be my witness!' he cried—'that when I heard his plan I thought it would be well! I thought that all the world would see we had not worshipped the Divine Man in vain! Pride in His glory, love for His Name, and ignorance of destiny,—these were the sins of Judas Iscariot,—but there was no malice in him, that I swear! The wretched youth's ambition for his Master was his ruin — but of us separate twain I was the faithless one!—Judas, even in his fault, was nevertheless faithful! Dost thou hear me, thou silent dreamer out of Egypt?' and he flashed a wild glance at the quiet Melchior; 'Dost thou hear? Write it if thou wilt on granite tablets in thy mystic land of the moon,—for I will have it known! Judas was faithful, I say!—and he loved the Lord better than any one of us all!'

'I hear thy words, Peter'—said Melchior gently— 'and I shall remember their purport.'

Calmed by the soft reply, the unhappy disciple recovered in part his self-possession, and went on with the coherent sequence of his narrative.

'Yea, in all things Judas was faithful. When he came first to confide in me, he told me that the chief priests and elders of the city were full of wrath and fear at the sway our Master had obtained over the minds of the people, and that they sought some excuse to kill Him. "Then let us away," said I. "Let us return unto the mountains, and the shores of Galilee, where our beloved Lord can teach His followers, unmolested, and at liberty." "Nay!" returned Judas in a voice of triumph—"Knowest thou not that if His words be true, our Lord can never die? Wherefore, why should we be driven from the city as though we were affrighted concerning His safety? Hear first what my sister Judith saith." And I did hear.'

Barabbas looked up, his eyes gleaming with anxiety and foreboding. Peter met his gaze mournfully.

'She—Judith—so I learned,—had welcomed her errant brother with such tenderness as moved his heart. She reproached him not at all, but listened with a patient interest to the story of his wanderings. Then she most gently said she doubted not the truth of the Divinity dwelling within the famous

"Nazarene," but surely, she argued, it were not un-
reasonable to ask that such Divinity be proved?
Whereat Judas, troubled in spirit, replied—"Verily
it hath been proved oftentimes by many marvellous
miracles." "Not in Jerusalem,—not to the priests
and rulers"—answered Judith. "For they believe
nothing of thy Prophet of Galilee, save that He
is a false blasphemer, a malcontent and traitor.
Nevertheless if He be of supreme omnipotence as
thou dost say, Judas, 'tis thou canst make Him seize
at once the mastery of the world,—and thus how
grandly thou wilt prove thy love!" Judas, entranced
at the boldness of this thought, bade her tell him
how such glory for his Lord might speedily be won.
"Never was task more easy"—she replied—"Resign
Him to the law,—betray Him to the priests! Then
will He avow His godhead with all the majesty of
Heaven! We shall acclaim Him as the true
Messiah,—and not we alone, but every nation of
the earth must worship Him! For bethink thee,
dearest brother, if He be indeed Divine, He cannot
be slain by any earthly foe!" This,' continued Peter,
'is what Judas told me of his sister's word. And,

at the time, it seemed both wise and just. For why should our great Lord suffer poverty and pain when empires could be His? Why should He wander homeless through the world, when all the palaces of earth should open to His coming? So Judas thought,—and I thought with him,—for the Master being in all things glorious, we saw no wrong in striving to make His glory manifest.'

'Nature's symbols are hard to read, Peter,' said Melchior suddenly—'And of a truth thou canst not comprehend their mystic lettering! What glory has ever yet been rendered "manifest" except through suffering? How could'st thou think to fit the tawdry splendours of earthly kingdoms to the embodied Spirit of the Divine? What throned and jewelled potentate hath ever lifted from the world a portion of its weight of sin? What name applauded by the people, hath ever yet bestowed salvation on a living soul? Lo, the very prophets of thy race have prophesied to thee in vain,—and to thy scared wits the oldest oracles lack meaning! Did not thy Master tell thee of His fate, and could'st thou not believe even Him?'

Peter grew very pale, and his head drooped on his breast.

'Yea, He did tell me'—he answered sorrowfully—'And I rebuked Him! I! I said—"This shall not be." And with all the wrath of a wronged King He turned upon me, saying "*Get thee behind Me, Satan! —for thou savourest not the things that be of God, but the things that be of men.*" And I fell back from Him affrighted, and was sore at heart all day!'

Melchior left his position by the palm-tree, and advancing, laid one hand on the disciple's arm.

'And thou could'st not realise, weak soul, these "things that be of God"?' he queried gravely—'Thou could'st not detach thy thoughts from earth? earth's paltry power and foolish flaunting ostentation? Alas for thee and those that take thee for a guide! for verily this fatal clinging of thy soul to things *temporal* shall warp thy way for ever and taint thy mission!'

Peter rose from his seat gazing at the speaker in wonder and dread. The moonlight fell on both their faces;—Melchior's was calm, stern and resolved,—Peter's expressed the deepest agitation.

'In God's name who art thou?' he asked apprehensively—'By whose authority dost thou prophesy concerning me?'

Melchior answered not.

'None shall take *me* for guide!' went on Peter more excitedly — 'For do I not confess myself a faulty man and spiritless? Moreover I am subject to temptations'—and he shuddered—'temptations many and grievous. Lo, the Master knew this of me, — for last night — only last night He said unto me — "*Simon, Simon, Satan hath desired to have thee that he may sift thee even as wheat. But I have prayed for thee that thy faith fail not*"'——

'And neither shall it fail!' interrupted Melchior solemnly—'By faith alone the fabric raised upon thy name shall live! Nevertheless thy cowardice and fears shall live on also, and thy lie shall be the seed from whence shall grow harvests of error! The law of compensation weighs on thee even as on every man, and thy one negation, Petrus, shall be the cause of many!'

Peter looked at the dark inscrutable countenance that confronted him, and lifted his hands as though

to ward off some menacing destiny. He trembled
violently.

'Strange prophet, thou dost fill my soul with
terrors!' he faltered—'What have I to do with those
that shall come after me? Surely when these days
are remembered, so will my sin be known and evermore accursed,—and who would raise a fabric, as
thou sayest, on the memory of a lie? Nay, nay!—
prophesy if thou wilt, good or evil, an' thou must
needs prophesy—but not here—not in this place
where the Master sat so lately. It is as though He
heard us—there is something of His presence in the
air!'

He cast a timorous glance up and down, and then
began to walk forward feebly yet hurriedly. They
all three paced along the moonlit road, Barabbas
casting many a dubious side-look at the worn and
troubled face of the disciple.

'Strange that this man could have denied his
Master!' he thought with passionate scorn—'And
I,—base sinner as I am, having but seen that
Master once, would willingly have died for Him
had it been possible! If all His followers are of

such coward stuff as' this, surely the history of
this day, if left to them, will be but a perverted
chronicle!'

Meanwhile, after a heavy pause, Peter resumed his
interrupted narrative.

'When Judas told me of his sister's words, methought I saw new light break in upon our lives.
The world would be a paradise,—all men would be
united in love and brotherhood if once the God on
earth were openly revealed! Yet out of fear I hesitated to pronounce a judgment; and seeing this,
Judas persuaded me to go with him to Judith and
hear her speak upon the matter. So, he said, I
should be better skilled to reason without haste or
prejudice.'

Here he threw up his hands with a wild gesture.

'Would I had never seen her!' he cried—'In what
a fair disguise the fiend did come to tempt my soul!
I took her for an angel of good counsel!—her beauty,
her mild voice, her sweet persuasions, her seeming-
wise suggestions, oh, they made havoc of my better
thoughts! She stood before us in her father's
garden, clothed softly in pure white, a very spirit of

gentleness and quietude, speaking full soberly and
with most excellent justice as I deemed. "Truly I
doubt not that this Lord of thine is very God," she
said—"Nevertheless as the rulers of the city believe
Him naught but human perjurer and traitor, ye who
love Him should compel Him to declare His glory.
For if He be not, as He saith, Divine, ye do wrong to
follow a deceiver. Surely this thing is plain? If
He be God, we all will worship Him; if He be man
only, why then ye are but blindly led astray, and
made as fools by trickery." Thus did she speak, and
I believed her,—her words seemed full of truth and
justice, — she was right, I said, — our Master was
Divine, and He should prove it! Smiling, she
bowed her head and left us,—and Judas, turning on
me, cried—"Now, Simon Peter, what thinkest thou?"
And I answering, said "Do as it seemeth well unto
thee, Judas! Our Lord is Lord of the whole heaven
and earth, and none can injure Him or take away
His glory!"'

Pausing again, he looked upward with a sad, wild
anguish, the pale moonbeams falling coldly on his
tear-worn, rugged countenance.

II.—6

'What counsel could I give?' he exclaimed, as though he were defending himself to some unseen listener in the starry skies—'What did I know? I had no key to heaven's mysteries! A poor unlearned fisherman, casting my nets by Galilee, was I, when He, the Marvellous One, came suddenly upon me, and with a lightning-glance of power said "*Follow Me!*" Andrew, my brother, was with me, and he will testify of this,—that we were ignorant and stricken by poverty, and all we knew and felt was that this Jesus of Nazareth must be obeyed,—that we were bound by some mysterious influence to follow where He led,— that home and kindred were as nought to us, compared with one smile, one searching look from Him! In beauty, in majesty, in high command a very King He seemed; why, why should not the world have known it? It seemed but natural,—it seemed but just, —and last night, when Judas rose from supper and went out, I knew whither he had gone! I knew—I knew!' He shuddered and groaned, — then with a savage gesture cried—'A curse on woman! Through her came sin and death!—through her is hell created!— through her is now betrayed the Holy One of God!

Accursëd may she be for ever!—and cursëd be all men who love her perishable beauty, and trust her treacherous soul!'

His white face became contorted with fury;—Melchior surveyed him with calm compassion.

'Thy curses are in vain, Petrus,'—he said—'They do but sound on deaf and empty air. He who curses woman or despises her, must henceforth be himself despisëd and accursëd. For now by woman's purity is the whole world redeemed,—by woman's tenderness and patience the cords of everlasting love are tied between this earth and highest heaven! Truly the language of symbols is hid from thee, if thou canst curse woman, remembering that of woman thy Master was born into the world! Were there a million treacherous women meriting thy curse, it matters little,—for from henceforward Womanhood is rendered sacred in the sight of the Eternal, through Her whom now we call the Mother of the " Nazarene "!'

He paused,— then added, 'Moreover, thou canst not fasten the betrayal of thy Lord on Judith Iscariot. Partly she was to blame,—yet she was but a tool in

the hands of the true arch-traitor.   If ye would track
treachery home to its very source, search for it where
it hath its chief abiding-place,—in the dens of priestcraft and tyranny,— among the seeming holy, the
seeming sanctified,—they with whom lies are part of
sacred office!'

Barabbas started.

''Twas Caiaphas?' he cried excitedly—' Tell me—
such news will be some comfort to my soul—'twas
Caiaphas who first did scheme this murder of the
Christ?'

Melchior looked at him steadily.

'Even so'—he said—''Twas Caiaphas.   What
would'st thou? 'Tis ever, and 'twill ever be, a self-
professing Priest of the Divine who crucifies
Divinity!'

XXIII

AS he spoke a faint wind stirred the shrubs and
trees on either side of the road like an assent-
ing sigh from some wandering spirit. The disciple
Peter stared upon him in troubled and vague
amazement.

'How could it be Caiaphas?' he asked—'True
it is that Judas went to Caiaphas, but not till
he had himself resolved upon the deed he meant
to do.'

'Thou knowest not each private detail of this
history, Petrus'—answered Melchior,—'And as thou
knowest not all, neither will they who come after thee
ever know. Hast thou not heard of love existing
between man and woman,—or if not love, a passion
passing by that name, which hath made many strange
annals in history? Even such passion has there

been 'twixt haughty Caiaphas and wanton Judith,—
nay, thou misguided Barabbas, wince not nor groan
—'tis true! To her the sensual priest confided all his
plan; he trained her in the part she had to play,—
by his command and in his very words she did
persuade and tempt her credulous brother,—yea, even
with a seeming excellent purpose in the work, to
bring back Judas to his home and the religion of his
fathers. Moreover, for her ready help and willingness
she did receive much gold from Caiaphas, and jewels
and soft raiment, things that such women love far
more than virtue. "Trap me the Nazarene, fair
Judith," he said, "with such discretion and wise
subtilty that it shall seem not my work but thy
brother's act of conscience and repentance to his faith
and people, and I will give thee whatsoever most thy
heart desires." And well did she obey him; as why
should she not?—seeing he long hath been her lover.'

Barabbas shrank back trembling. Every instinct
in him told him it was the truth he heard, yet he
could not bear to have it thus pitilessly thrust upon
him. Meanwhile the unhappy Simon Peter wrung
his hands together in desperation.

'Nay, who could guess so deep and dastardly a
plot!' he cried—'And if thou knewest it, thou fateful
stranger, and wert in Jerusalem, why not have given
us warning?'

'Of what profit would have been my words?'
demanded Melchior with sudden scorn—'Ye would
not believe the sayings of your Master,—how then
should ye believe me? Ye were and are, the very
emblems of mankind, self-seeking, doubting and
timorous,—and gloze it over as ye will, ye were
all unfaithful and afraid! As for me, 'tis not my
creed to strive and turn the course of destiny. I say
the priests have killed the Christ; and the great
Murder is not yet finished. For they will kill Him
spiritually a million times again ere earth shall fully
comprehend the glory of His message. Ay!—
through the vista of a thousand coming years and
more, I see His silent patient Figure stretched upon
the Cross, and ever the priests surround Him, driving
in the nails!' He paused, and his dark eyes flashed
with a strange fierce passion,—then he continued
quietly—''Tis so ordained. Lo, yonder are the
shadows of Gethsemane,—if thou hast aught of

import more to say of Judas,—it were well to speak it here—and now—ere we go further.'

Instinctively he lowered his voice, — and with equal instinctiveness, all three men drew closer together, the moonlight casting lengthened reflections of their draped figures on a smooth piece of sun-dried turf which sloped in undulating lines down towards a thicket of olive-trees, glimmering silver-grey in the near distance. Peter trembled as with icy cold, and looked timorously backward over his shoulder with the manner of one who expects to see some awful presence close behind him.

'Yea,—out of justice to the dead,—out of pure justice'—he muttered faintly—'ye should know all of Judas that my faltering tongue can tell. For of a truth his end is horrible! 'Twas a brave youth, comely and bold, and warm and passionate,—and to die thus alone—down there in the darkness!' . . . Clenching his fists hard, he tried to control his nervous shuddering, and went on, speaking in low troubled tones,—'I said he went to Caiaphas. This was two nights before our last supper with the Lord. He told

me all. Caiaphas feigned both anger and indifference.
"We have no fear of thy mad fanatic out of Galilee"
—he said—"but if thy conscience do reproach thee,
Judas, as well it may, for thy desertion of the law and
the faith of thine own people, we will not discourage
or reject thy service. Yet think not thou canst
arrogantly place the Sanhedrim under any personal
obligation for thine offered aid,—the priests elect
may take no favours from one who hath perversely
deserted the holy rites of God, and hath forsaken the
following of his fathers. Understand well, we cannot
owe thee gratitude ; for thou hast severed thyself
wilfully from us and hast despised our high authority.
Wherefore if now thou art prepared to render up the
Man of Galilee, name thine own payment." Now
Judas had no thought of this, and being sorely
grieved, refused, and went away, stricken at heart.
And to his sister he declared all, and said—"I will
not sell the Lord into His glory for base coin." But
she made light of the matter and mocked at his
scruples. "Thou silly soul, thou dost not sell thy
Lord !" she said—"Thou dost merely enter into a
legal form of contract, which concerns thee little.

'Tis the Pharisaical rule of honour not to accept
unpaid service from one who doth openly reject the
faith. Take what they offer thee,—canst thou not
use it for the sick and poor? Remember thou art
serving thy Master,—thou dost not 'sell' or otherwise betray Him. Thy work prepares Him to avow
His glory!—think what a marvel thou wilt thus reveal
to all the world! Hesitate not therefore for a mere
scribe's formula." Then Judas, thus persuaded, went
again to Caiaphas, saying " Truly ye have your laws
with which I have naught in common, yet if it must
be so, *what will ye give me if I betray Him unto
you?*" And straightway they counted from the
treasury thirty pieces of silver, which Judas took
unwillingly. Alas, alas! If he had only known!
Surely this very money was as a blind for Caiaphas,
—a seeming legal proof that he was innocent of
treachery,—but that, in custom of the law, he paid the
voluntary, self-convicted traitor. Who could accuse
Caiaphas of cruelty?—of malice?—of intent to
murder? Caiaphas was not paid! All things con-
spired to fix the blame on Judas,—to make him bear
alone that awful weight of crime, which heavier than

all burdens of despair, hath sunk him now within the depths of hell.'

He pressed his hands upon his forehead for a moment and was silent. Barabbas watched him gloomily, absorbed in his every gesture, his every word,—Melchior's eyes were cast down, and a stern expression shadowed his features, notwithstanding that every incident of the story seemed known to him.

'The end came quickly'—proceeded the disciple, after a sorrowful pause—'All the misery and fury and despair fell upon us in one blow. The haste and anger of the law swept down upon us like a storm which we had neither force nor valour to resist. At the entrance to the garden of Gethsemane, Judas waited, with glare of torches and armed men,—and as the Lord came forth from out of the shadows of the trees, he went to meet Him. Pale with expected triumph, love and fear, he cried " *Hail, Master!* " and kissed Him. And such a silence fell upon us all that methought the very earth had stopped its course, and that all the stars were listening! Now, thought I, will the glory of the God expand!—and even as we saw Him transfigured on the mountain, so will He

shine in splendour, mighty and terrible, and over-
whelm His enemies as with fire! But He, the Master,
changed not in aught, nor spoke; in stillness and in
patience He fixed His eyes on Judas for a while—
then in low tones He said—"*Friend, wherefore art
thou come? Betrayest thou the Son of Man with a
kiss?*" And Judas, with a cry of anguish, fell back
from Him affrighted, and clutched at my garments,
whispering—"Surely I have sinned!—or else He
hath deceived us!" Meanwhile the armed guards
stood mute as slaves, not offering to touch the Lord,
till He, addressing them, said—"*Whom seek ye?*"
Then they, abashed, did answer—"Jesus of Nazareth."
Whereupon the Master looked upon them straightly,
saying "*I am He.*" Then, as though smitten by
thunder at these words, they went backward and fell
to the ground. And I, foolishly, thought the hour
we waited for had come,—for never did such
splendour, such dignity and power appear in mortal
frame as at that moment glorified our Lord. Again
He spoke unto the guard, saying "*Whom seek ye?*"
And again they answered trembling, "*Jesus of
Nazareth.*" Then said He tranquilly—"*I have told*

ye that I am He. If therefore ye seek Me, let these go their way." And turning upon us slowly, He waved His hand in parting,—a kingly sign of proud and calm dismissal. Staring upon Him, as though He were a vision, we retreated from His path, while He did royally advance and render Himself up to those who sought Him. And these, in part recovered from their fear, laid hold on Him and led Him away. We,—we His disciples gazed after Him a while, then gazing on each other, raved and wept. "Deceived! Deceived!" we cried—"He is not God but man!" And then we fled, each on our separate ways,—and only I, moved by desire to see the end, followed the Master afar off, even unto the very house of Caiaphas.'

Here Peter stopped, overcome by agitation. Tears sprung to his eyes and choked his voice, but presently mastering himself with an effort, he said hoarsely, and in ashamed accents,—

'There I did deny Him! I confess it,—I denied Him. When the chattering slaves and servants of the high-priest declared I was His disciple, I swore, and said "I know not the man!" And after all

'twas true,—'twas true! I knew not the "man,"—
for I had known, or thought that I had known,
the God!'

Melchior raised his piercing dark eyes, and studied
him closely.

'Thus dost thou play the sophist!' he said with
chill disdain—'Thus wilt thou bandy reasons and
excuses for thine own sins and follies! Weak,
cowardly, and moved by the desire of temporal
shows, thou wilt invent pardon for thine own blindness thus for ever! Thou art the perfect emblem
of thy future fame! If thou hadst truly known the
God, thou could'st not have denied Him,—but if
thou wilt speak truth, Petrus, thou never hast believed
in Him, save as a possible earthly King, who might
in time possess Jerusalem. To that hope thou didst
cling,—and of things heavenly thou hadst no comprehension. To possess the earth has ever been thy
dream!—maybe thou wilt possess it, thou and thy
followers after thee,—but Heaven is far distant from
thy ken!' Peter's face flushed, and his eyes
glittered with something like anger.

'Thou dost judge me harshly, stranger'—he said.

'Nevertheless perchance thou hast some justice in thy words. Yet surely 'tis not unnatural to look for glory from what is glorious? If God be God, why should He not declare Himself?—if He be ruler of the earth, why should not His sway be absolute and visible?'

'He doth declare Himself—His sway is absolute and visible!' said Melchior,—'But thou art not His medium, Petrus!—nor doth He stoop from highest Heaven to learn earth's laws from thee.'

Peter was silent. Barabbas now looked at him with renewed curiosity,—he was beginning to find out the singular and complex character of the man. Cowardice and dignity, terror and anger, remorse and pride all struggled together in his nature, and even the untutored Barabbas could see that from this timorous disciple anything in the way of shiftiness or subterfuge might be expected, since he was capable of accusing and excusing himself of sin at one and the same time.

'Say what thou wilt' he resumed, with a touch of defiance in his manner—''twas the chagrin and the bitter disappointment of my soul that caused me to

deny the "Man." I was aflame with eagerness to
hail the God!—'twould have been easy for Him to
declare His majesty, and yet, before the minions of
the law He held His peace! His silence and His
patience maddened me!—and when He passed out
with the guard and looked at me, I wept,—not only
for my own baseness, but for sheer wretchedness at
His refusal to reveal Himself to men. Meanwhile,
as He was led away to Pontius Pilate, Judas, furious
with despair, rushed into the presence of Caiaphas,
and there before him and other of the priests and
elders cried aloud — "*I have sinned, in that I have
betrayed the innocent blood!*" And they, jeering at
him, laughed among themselves, and answered him
saying "*What is that to us? See thou to that!*"
Whereat he flung down all the silver they had given
him on the floor before them and departed,—and as
he ran from out the palace like a man distraught, I
met and stopped him. "Judas, Judas, whither goest
thou?" I cried. He beat me off. "Home! Home!"
he shrieked at me—"Home—to *her!*—to the one
sister whom I loved, who did persuade my soul to
this night's treachery! Let me pass!—for I must

curse her ere I die!—her spirit needs must follow mine to yonder beckoning Doom!" And with a frightful force he tore himself from out my grasp, and like a drifting phantom on the wind, was gone!'

Here Peter raised his hands with an eloquent gesture, as though he again saw the vanishing form of the despairing man.

'All through last night,' he continued in hushed accents — 'I sought for him in vain. Round and about Iscariot's house I wandered aimlessly,—I saw none of whom I dared ask news of him,—the fatal garden where together we had speech with Judith, was silent and deserted. Through many streets of the city, and along the road to Bethany I paced wearily, until at last some fateful spirit turned my steps towards Gethsemane. And there,—there at last—I found him!'

He paused,—then suddenly began to walk rapidly.

'Come!' he said, looking backward at Melchior and Barabbas—'Come! The night advances,—and he hath passed already many lonely hours! And not long since the Master said—"*Greater love hath no man than this,—that a man lay down his life for*

his friends." Verily Judas hath laid down his life,
—and look you, to die thus in the full prime of
youth, strangled even as a dog that hath run wild,
is horrible!—will't not suffice? 'Twere hard that
Judas should be evermore accursed, seeing that for
his folly he hath paid the utmost penalty, and is, by
his own hand, dead!'

'And thou livest!' said Melchior with a cold
smile—'Thou sayest well, Petrus;—'twere hard that
Judas should be evermore accursed and thou adjudged
a true apostle! Yet such things happen—for the
world loves contrarys and falsifications of history,—
and while perchance it takes a month to spread a
lie, it takes a hundred centuries to prove a truth!'

Peter answered not,—he was pressing on with in-
creasing speed and agitation. All at once he halted,
—the road made an abrupt slope towards a mass of
dense foliage faintly grey in the light of the moon.

'Hush!—hush!' he whispered—'He is dead,—but
there is a strange expression in his eyes,—he looks
as if he heard. One cannot tell,—the dead may hear
for all we know! Tread gently,—yonder is the
garden of Gethsemane, but he is not within it. He

stays outside,—almost upon the very spot where he did give the Master up to death, meaning to give Him glory! Come!—we will persuade him to depart with us,—betwixt us three he shall be gently carried home,—perchance his sister Judith marvels at his absence, and waits for his return! How she will smile upon him when she sees the manner of his coming!'

And he began to walk forward on tip-toe. Barabbas grew deadly pale and caught Melchior by the arm. The rugged figure of the disciple went on before them like a dark fluttering shadow, and presently turned aside from the road towards a turfy hollow where a group of ancient olive-trees stretched out their gaunt black branches like spectral arms uplifted to warn intruders back. Pausing at this gloomily frondaged portal, Peter beckoned his companions with a solemn gesture,—then, stooping under the boughs, he passed and disappeared. Hushing their footsteps and rendered silent by the sense of awe, Melchior and Barabbas followed. The hanging foliage drooped over them heavily, and seemed to draw them in and close them out of sight,

—and although there was scarcely any wind to move the air, the thick leaves rustled mysteriously like ghostly voices whispering of some awful secret known to them alone—the secret of a tortured soul's remorse, —the indescribable horror of a sinner's death, self-sought in the deeper silence of their sylvan shadows.

XXIV

MEANWHILE the city of Jerusalem was pleasantly astir. Lights twinkled from the windows of every house, and from many an open door and flower-filled garden came the sounds of music and dancing. Those who had been well-nigh dead with fear at the earthquake and the unnatural darkness of the day, were now rejoicing at the safety of themselves and their relations. No more cause for apprehension remained; the night was cloudlessly beautiful, and brilliant with the tranquil glory of the nearly full moon, — and joyous parties of friends assembled together without ceremony to join in merriment and mutual congratulation. The scene on Calvary was the one chief topic of conversation,— every tongue discoursed eloquently upon the heroic death of the 'Nazarene.' All agreed that never was so beautiful a Being seen in mortal mould, or one more brave, or royal of aspect,—nevertheless it was also the general opinion that it was well He was dead. There was no doubt but that He would have been dangerous,—He advanced Himself as a reformer, and His teachings were decidedly set against both the realm's priestcraft and policy. Moreover it was evident that He possessed some strange interior power,—He had genius too, that strong and rare quality which draws after it all the lesser and weaker spirits of men,—it was well and wise that He was crucified! People who had travelled as far as Greece and Rome, shook their heads and spoke profoundly of 'troublesome philosophers,' they who insisted on truth as a leading principle of life, and objected to shams.

'This Galilean was one of their kind'—said a meditative old scribe, standing at his house-door to chat with a passing acquaintance,—'Save that He spoke of a future life and an eternal world, He could say no better and no more than they. Surely there are stories enough of Socrates to fill one's mouth,— he was a man for truth also, and was for ever thus upsetting laws, wherefore they killed him. But he was old, and the " Nazarene " was young,—and death in youth is somewhat piteous. All the same 'tis better so, — for look you, He ran wild with prophecy on life eternal. Heaven defend us all, say I, from any other world save this one! — this is enough for any man — and were there yet another to inherit, 'tis certain we are not fitted for it; we die, and there's an end,—no man ever rose from the dead.'

'Hast thou heard it said'—suggested his friend hesitatingly, 'that this same " Nazarene " declared that He would rise again?'

The old scribe smiled contemptuously.

'I have heard many things'—he answered,—'but because I hear, I am not compelled to believe. And of all the follies ever spoken this is the greatest. No doubt the Galilean's followers would steal His body if they could, and swear He had arisen from the dead,—but the high-priest Caiaphas hath had a warning, and he will guard against deception. Trouble not thyself with such rumours,—a dead man, even a prophet of God, is dead for ever.'

And he went in and shut his door, leaving his acquaintance to go on his way homeward, which that personage did somewhat slowly and thoughtfully.

All the streets of the city were bathed in a silver-clear shower of moonbeams,—the air was balmy and scented with the fragrance of roses and orange-boughs,—groups of youths and maidens sauntered here and there in the cool of the various gardens, laughing, chatting, and now and then lifting up their well-attuned voices in strophes of choral song. Jerusalem basked in the soft radiance of the Eastern night like a fairy city of pleasure, and there was no sign among her joyous people to show that the Redeemer of the world had died for the world's sake that day.

In marked contrast to the animation prevailing in other streets and courts, a great stillness surrounded the house of Pontius Pilate, the Roman governor. The fountain in the outer colonnade alone made music to itself as it tossed up its delicate dust-like spray that fell tinkling back again into the marble basin,—no wandering breeze ruffled the petals of the white roses that clung like little bunches of crumpled

silk to the dark walls,—even the thirsty and monotonous chirp-chirping of the locusts had ceased.
Now and then a servant crossed the court on some
errand, with noiseless feet,—and one Roman soldier
on guard paced slowly to and fro, his sandals making
scarcely any sound as he measured his stately march
forward a dozen lengths or so, then backward, then
forward again, the drooping pennon on his lifted
lance throwing a floating snake-like shadow behind
him as he moved. Pilate, since the morning, had
been seriously indisposed, and all his retinue were
more or less uneasy. Quiet had been enforced upon
the household by its haughty and resolute mistress,—
and now that night had fallen the deep hush seemed
likely to be unbroken till a new day should dawn.
So that when a loud and urgent knocking was
heard at the outmost gate, the porter who opened
it was almost speechless with indignation and
amazement.

'I prithee cease thy rude clamour'—he said, after
he had looked out of his loophole of observation and
seen that the would-be intruder was a man of dis-
tinguished appearance and attire—'Thou canst not

enter here with all thy knocking,—the governor is ill and sees no man.'

'Nevertheless I must have speech with him,' responded the visitor—'I do beseech thee, friend, delay me not—my matter presses.'

'I tell thee 'tis not possible'—said the porter— 'Would'st have us lose our heads for disobeying orders? Or crucified even as the "Nazarene"?'

'My business doth concern the "Nazarene"'—was the reply, given hurriedly and with evident emotion— 'Tell this to one in authority, and say that 'tis Joseph of Arimathea who waits without.'

At these words the porter ceased arguing, and disappeared across the court into the house. Presently he returned, accompanied by a tall slave, wearing a silver chain of office.

'Worthy Counsellor'—said this retainer, respectfully saluting the Arimathean,—'Thou canst not at this late hour have speech with Pilate, who hath been sorely overwrought by the harassments of the day,—but I am commanded by the lady Justitia to say that she will receive thee willingly if indeed thy matter is of the Man of Nazareth.'

'It is—it is'—answered Joseph eagerly—'I do entreat thee, bring me to thy lady straight, for every moment lost doth hinder the fulfilment of mine errand.'

The slave said no more, but signed to the porter to unbar the gate with as little noise as possible. Then he led the way across the court, gave a word of explanation to the soldier on guard, and finally escorted the visitor into an arched vestibule adorned with flowering plants, and cooled by sparkling jets of water that ran from carved lions' mouths into a deep basin of yellow marble. Here the slave disappeared, leaving the Arimathean alone. He paced up and down with some impatience, full of his own burning thoughts that chafed at every fresh delay, and he was violently startled when a grave mellow voice said close to him,

'What of the Christ? Have ye indeed slain Him?'

'Lady!' . . . he stammered, and turned to confront the wife of Pilate, who had silently entered the vestibule behind him. For a moment he could find no words wherewith to answer her,—the steadfastness of her dark eyes troubled him. She was beautiful in a grand and stately way,—her resolute features and brooding brows expressed more fierceness than tenderness, and yet her lips quivered with some deeply suppressed emotion as she spoke again and said—

'Surely thou art a Jew, and hast had thy share in this murder?'

With the shock of this bitterly pronounced accusation he recovered his self-possession.

'Noble Justitia, I beseech thee in the name of God number me not with the evil ones of this misguided nation!' he answered passionately—'Could I have saved the heaven-born "Nazarene," surely I would have given my own life willingly! For I have gathered profit from His holy doctrine, and am His sworn disciple, though secretly, for fear of the harshness of mine own people, who would cast me out from their midst if they knew the change wrought within my soul. Moreover I am a man who hath studied the sayings of the prophets, not lightly but with sober judgment, and do accept all the things that now have chanced to us as fulfilment of the word of

God. And most heartily do I render thanks unto the Most High that He hath in His great mercy permitted me to see with mortal eyes His chosen true Messiah!'

'Thou dost then freely acknowledge Him as One Divine?' said Justitia, fixing a searching look upon him.

'Most surely, lady! If ever any god did dwell on earth, 'twas He.'

'Then He lives yet?'

Joseph looked perplexed and troubled.

'Nay! He is dead. Hath He not been crucified?'

'Doth a god die?' asked Justitia, her sombre eyes glittering strangely — 'What power have mortal tortures on immortal spirit? Summon thy reason and think calmly—art sure that He is dead?'

Her words and manner were so solemn and impressive that the Arimathean counsellor was for a moment bewildered and amazed, and knew not what to say. Then, after a doubtful pause, he answered,

'Lady, as far as human eye and sense can judge,

life hath verily departed from Him. His body hath been taken down from off the Cross, and for the reason that they found Him dead, they have spared the breaking of His limbs. Whereas the malefactors that were crucified with Him have had their joints twisted and snapt asunder lest haply any spark of pained existence should linger in them yet. But He of Nazareth having perished utterly, and no faint pulse of blood being feebly astir in any portion of His matchless frame, the men of the law have judged it politic and merciful to give His mortal pure remains to her who bore Him,—Mary, His sorrowing Mother, who weeps beside Him now.'

Justitia heard, and her pale resolute face grew paler.

'Is't possible Divinity can perish?' she murmured. Again she looked steadily, searchingly at the thoughtful and earnest countenance of the Arimathean, and added, with a touch of the domineering haughtiness which made her name a terror to her household,— 'Then, Counsellor Joseph, if thy words be true, and the Galilean Prophet be no longer living, what can thine errand be concerning Him?'

''Tis naught but one of simple duty to the noble

dead '—he replied quickly, and with anxiety—' I fain would bury the body of the Lord where it may be most reverently shrined and undisturbed. There is a sepulchre newly hewn among the rocks outside the city, not far from Calvary, but going downwards towards Gethsemane,—'twas meant for mine own tomb, for well I know the years advance with me, and only God knoweth how soon I may be called upon to die,—nevertheless if I may lay the body of the Master therein, I shall be well content to be interred in baser ground below Him. We would not have Him sepulchred with common malefactors, — wherefore, noble lady, I seek thy lord the governor's permission to place within this unused burial cave of mine own choosing and purchase, the sacred corpse of One who, to my thinking, was indeed the Christ, albeit He hath been crucified. This is my errand,—and I have sped hither in haste to ask from Pilate his free and favour- able consent, which, if it be granted, will make of me a grateful debtor to the gentleness of Rome.'

Justitia smiled darkly at the courteous phrase 'the gentleness of Rome,'—then her fierce brows con- tracted in a puzzled line.

'Truly I know not how to aid thee, friend,'—she said after a pause—'I have no power to grant thee this permit,—and my lord is sorely wearied and distempered by strange fancies and—dreams,—unhappy and confusing dreams,'—she repeated slowly and with a slight shudder—'Yet—stay! Wait but one moment,—I will inquire of him his mood,—perchance it may relieve him to have speech with thee.'

Gliding away on her noiseless sandalled feet, her majestic figure in its trailing robes of white glimmered in and out the marble columns of the corridor and rapidly disappeared. Joseph of Arimathea sighed heavily, and stood looking vaguely at the trickling water running from the mouths of the stone lions into the marble-lined hollow in the centre of the vestibule, wondering to himself why his heart had beat so violently, and why his thoughts had been so suddenly troubled when he had been asked the question, 'Art sure that He is dead?' He was not left long alone to indulge in his reflections,—Justitia returned almost as quickly as she had vanished, and pausing at a little distance beckoned to him.

'Pilate will see thee'—she said, as he eagerly

obeyed her gesture—'But should'st thou find him wild and wandering in discourse, I pray thee heed him not. And beware how thou dost speak of his distemper to the curious gossips of the city,—I would not have it noised abroad that he hath been all day so far distracted from his usual self'—here her steady voice trembled and her proud eyes filled with sudden tears—' He hath been ill—very ill—and only I have tended him ; and notwithstanding he is calmer now, thou must in converse use discretion.'

'Trust me, noble lady'—replied the Arimathean with profound feeling, 'I will most faithfully endeavour that I shall not err in aught, or chafe thy lord with any new displeasure.'

She bent her haughty head, partly in acknowledgment of his words, partly to hide the tears that glittered on her lashes, and, without further parley, led the way to her husband's private room. In deep silence, hushing his footsteps heedfully as he moved, the Arimathean counsellor followed her.

XXV

PASSING through a narrow passage curtained off from the rest of the house, they entered a long low vaulted apartment brilliantly ablaze with lights. Roman lamps set on iron brackets illuminated every corner that would otherwise have been dark,— waxen torches flamed in every fixed sconce. There was so much flare, and faint smoke from burnt perfumes, that for a moment it was impossible to discern anything clearly, although the wide casement window was set open to the night, and steps led down from it to a closely-walled garden on which the moon poured refreshing showers of silver radiance, eclipsing all the artificial glamour and glare within. And at this casement, extended on a couch, lay Pilate, pallid and inert, with half-closed eyes, and limp hands falling on either side of the silken coverlet spread over him — he had the supine and passive air of a long-ailing, dying man to whom death would be release and blessedness. Joseph of Arimathea could scarcely restrain an exclamation of amazed compassion as he saw him,—but a warning glance from Justitia silenced him, and he repressed his feeling. She meanwhile went up to her husband's couch and knelt beside it.

'The counsellor is here, Pontius'—she said softly — 'Hast thou strength to give him audience?'

Pilate opened his eyes widely and stared vaguely at his visitor,—then lifting one hand that trembled in the air with weakness, beckoned him to approach.

'Come nearer,—nearer still'—he murmured with a kind of feeble pettishness,—'Thou hast the look of a shadow yonder,—the room is full of shadows. Thou art Joseph? From that city of the Jews called Arimathea?'

'Even so, my lord'—answered Joseph in subdued accents, noting with pained concern the Roman governor's prostrate and evidently suffering condition.

'And being a Jew, what dost thou seek of me?' went on Pilate, his heavy lids again half closing over his eyes—'Surely I have this day fully satisfied the Israelitish thirst for blood!'

'Most noble governor,' said Joseph, with as careful gentleness and humility as he could command—'Believe me that I am not one of those who forced thee to the deed 'twas evident thy spirit did repudiate and abhor. And albeit thou hast been named a tyrant and a cruel man by the unthinking of my nation, I know thy gentleness, having discovered much of thy good work in deeds of charity among the poor,—therefore I come to beg of thee the Body of the Christ'——

With a sudden excited movement, Pilate dashed aside the silken draperies that covered him, and sat up, nervously clutching his wife's arm.

'The Body of the Christ!' he echoed wildly—'Hearest thou that, Justitia! The Body of the Christ!'

His purple garments fell about him in disordered

folds,—his vest half open, showed his chest heaving
agitatedly with his unquiet and irregular breathing,—
his eyes grew feverishly luminous, and gleamed with
a strange restless light from under the shadow of his
tossed and tumbled hair. Joseph, alarmed at his
aspect, stood hesitating,—Justitia looked at him, and
made him a mute sign to go on and make his appeal
quickly.

'Yea, 'tis the Body of the Christ I ask from thee;'
he proceeded then, anxiously yet resolvedly—'And
verily I would not have troubled thee at this hour,
Pilate, but that thou art governor and ruler of the
civil laws within Judæa, therefore thou alone canst
give me that which hath been slain by law. I fain
would lay the sacred corpse within mine own new
sepulchre, with all the tears and prayers befitting a
great hero dead.'

'Dead?' cried Pilate, fixing a wild stare upon him,
'Already dead? Nay—art thou sure?'

A chill tremor shook the strong nerves of the
Arimathean. Here was the same question Justitia
had asked him a few minutes since,—and it aroused
the same strange trouble in his mind. And while he

stood amazed, unable to find words for an immediate response, Pilate sprang erect, tossing his arms up like a man distraught.

'Dead!' he cried again. 'O fools, fools, whose sight is so deceived! No mortal power can slay the "Nazarene,"—He lives and He hath always lived! Yea, from the beginning even unto the end, if any end there be! What?—ye have crucified Him?—ye have seen His flesh pierced, and His blood flow? Ye have touched Him?—ye have seen Him share in mortal labours, mortal woes and mortal needs,—ye have proved Him made of perishable fleshly stuff that ye can torture and destroy?—O poor dim-sighted fools! Lo, ye have done the bravest and most wondrous deed that ever was inscribed in history,—ye have crucified a Divine Appearance!—ye have gloated over the seeming death of the Deathless! A God was with us,—wearing apparent mortal vesture, but those who saw the suffering Man and Man alone, did only *think* they saw! I looked beyond,—I, Pilate,—I beheld'— Here he broke off with a smothered exclamation, his eyes fixing themselves alarmedly upon the outer garden bathed in the full glory of the moon. 'Justitia! Justitia!' he cried.

She sprang to him,—and he caught her convulsively in his arms, drawing her head down against his bosom, and straining her to his heart with passionate violence.

'Hush!—hush!' he murmured,—'Let us not weep, — the thing is done, — remorse will not avail. Accursëd Jews!—they forced my hand,—they, with their devilish priest, did slay the Man, not I. "*Ecce Homo!*" I cried to them, — I sought to make them see even as I saw,—the glory, the terror, and the wonder,—the radiance of that seeming-human Form, so fine and marvellous, that methought it would have vanished into ether! Even as the lightning did He shine! His flesh was but a garment, transparent as a mist, through which one sees the sun! Nevertheless, let us not weep despairingly,—tears are but foolish—for He is not dead—He could not die, although He hath been crucified. He hath the secret clue of death;—'tis a mystery unfathomable, — for what the gods may mean by this we know not,—and what the world hath done we know not,—howbeit let the world look to it, for we are not to blame!' He paused, caressing with a sort of fierce tenderness the dark ripples of his wife's luxuriant hair. 'My love!' he said pityingly—'My poor, tired, anxious heart! No more tears, Justitia, I pray thee,—we will forget this day, for truly it concerns us not,—'tis the Jews' work,—let the Jews answer for it — for I will not; neither to Cæsar nor to God! I have said and still will say — *I am innocent of the blood of this just Man!*'

Here, loosening his arms suddenly from around his wife, he raised them with a proud and dignified gesture of protest,—then turning suddenly, and perceiving Joseph of Arimathea where he stood apart, a silent and troubled spectator of the scene, he advanced towards him, and said gently—

' Friend, what seekest thou of me ? '

The Arimathean cast a despairing glance of appeal at Justitia, who, hastily dashing away the tears on her cheeks, and mastering the emotion that betrayed itself in her pale and sorrowful countenance, came to his rescue.

'Dear lord, hast thou forgotten?' she said gently, as with a guiding movement of her hand she persuaded Pilate to resume his seat upon the couch near the open window—'Thou art not well, and the harassments of thy work have over-wearied thee. This man doth seek the body of the "Nazarene" for burial,—himself he charges with the duties of this office if thou wilt give him thy permit,—grant him his boon, I do beseech thee, and let him go his way, for thou must rest again and sleep — thou hast been sorely tried!'

Pilate sank heavily among his cushions, looking blankly into nothingness.

'Thou would'st bury the Christ?' he asked at last, speaking with difficulty, as though his tongue were stiff and refused utterance.

'Such is my one desire, my lord' — answered Joseph, hopefully now, for Pilate seemed more capable of reason.

'In thine own sepulchre?'

'Even there.'

''Tis large? Will't hold embodied Light and Life, and yet not rive asunder?'

'My lord!'— faltered the Arimathean, in dismay
and fear.

Justitia slipped one arm around her husband's
neck and said something to him in a soothing
whisper. Pilate smiled somewhat piteously, and
drawing her hand down to his lips kissed it.

'This gentle lady, — my wife, good sir,—tells me
that my thoughts wander, and that I fail to give thee
fitting answer. I crave thy pardon, counsellor,—
thou art a counsellor, it seems, and therefore no
doubt hast patience with the erring, and wisdom
for the weak. Thou would'st ensepulchre the
" Nazarene "?—the body of the Crucified thou would'st
number with dead men?—why then, even so let
it be!—Take thou possession of That which thou
dost deem a corpse of common clay,—thou hast my
leave to honourably inter the same. My leave!'
—and he laughed wildly—'My leave to shut within
the tomb That which no tomb can hold, no close-
barred cave can keep, no time destroy! Go!—
do as thou wilt,—do all thou wilt!—thou hast thy
boon!'

Relieved from his suspense, and full of gratitude,

the Arimathean bowed profoundly to the ground, and was about to retire, when a great noise of disputation was heard in the outer vestibule. Justitia started up from her husband's side in wondering indignation, and was on the point of going forth to inquire the cause of such unseemly disturbance, when the door of the apartment was furiously flung open, and the high-priest Caiaphas burst in, his glistening sacerdotal garments disordered and trailing behind him, and his face livid with passion.

'Thou art a traitor, Pilate!' he exclaimed—'Already dost thou scheme with tricksters for the pretended resurrection of the "Nazarene"!'

XXVI

PILATE rose slowly up and confronted him, Justitia at his side. He was now perfectly calm, and his pale features assumed a cold and repellent dignity.

'Whom callest thou traitor, thou subject of Rome?' he said—'Knowest thou not that though thou art high-priest of the Jewish faith, thou art answerable to Cæsar for insult to his officer?'

Caiaphas stood breathless and trembling with rage.

'Thou also art answerable to Cæsar if thou dost lend thyself to low imposture!' he said—'Dost thou not remember that this vile deceiver out of Galilee who hath been crucified did say "*After three days I will rise again*"? And do I not find thee giving audience to one of His known followers, who oft

hath entertained Him and listened to His doctrines?
This counsellor'—and he emphasised the term
sarcastically, eyeing the unmoved and stately figure
of Joseph of Arimathea up and down angrily—'now
seeks His body to bury it in a sepulchre, whereof he
only hath the seal and secret. And why doth he
offer this free service? That he may steal the corpse
in the silence of the second night, and make away
with it, and then give out a rumour that the Christ
is risen! *So shall the last error be worse than the first*
with the silly multitude, if his scheme be not
prevented.'

Joseph lifted his clear grave eyes and looked full
at the speaker.

'I heed not thy wicked accusation, Caiaphas'—he
said tranquilly—'Thou knowest it is false, and born
from out the fury and suspicion of thy mind. Thy
fears do make a coward of thee,—perchance when
thou didst find the veil of the Temple rent in the
midst this day, and knewest by inquiry that so it
had been torn at the very moment of the passing of
the soul of the "Nazarene," thou wert shaken with
strange terrors that still do haunt and trouble thee!

Rally thyself and be ashamed,—for none shall steal the body I have claimed from Pilate,—rest for the dead is granted even by the most unmerciful; and this rest is mine to give to One who, whether human or Divine, was innocent of sin, and died through treachery undeservedly.'

The blood rushed to the high-priest's brows, and he clenched his hands in an effort to keep down his rising wrath.

'Hearest thou that, Pilate?' he exclaimed— 'Sufferest thou this insolence?'

'What insolence?' asked Justitia suddenly—''Tis true the Man of Nazareth had no fault in Him at all, and that ye slew Him out of fear!'

Caiaphas glared at her, his cold eyes sparkling with rage.

'I argue not with women!' he said through his set teeth—'They are not in our counsels, nor have they any right to judgment.'

Justitia smiled. Her full black eyes met his piercing shallow ones with such immeasurable scorn as made him for the moment tremble. Avoiding her glance, he addressed himself once more to Pilate—

'Hear me, thou governor of Judæa under Cæsar,'—
he said—'And weigh thou this matter well lest thou
unheedfully fall beneath the weight of the Imperial
displeasure. Thy Roman soldiery are stricken with
some strange disease, and speak as with the milky
mouths of babes, concerning mercy!—'tis marvellous
to note yon bearded men seized with effeminate
virtue! Wherefore, out of this sudden craze of
mercy they have spared to break the limbs of the
blasphemous "Nazarene," proffering for excuse that
He is dead already. What matter! I would have
had every joint within His body wrenched apart!—
yea, I would have had His very flesh hewn into pieces
after death, if I had had my way!' He paused,
quivering with passion and breathing heavily. Pilate
looked at him with immovable intentness. 'Thy
centurion is at fault'—he continued—'for he it is
who hath, upon his own authority, given the corpse
unto the women who besought it of him, and they
make such a weeping and a lamentation as might
rouse the multitude, an' 'twere not that the hour is
late and night has fully fallen. And with them is
that evil woman of the town, the Magdalen, who

doth defy us to remove the body and place it as it should be, with the other malefactors, saying that this man '—and he indicated by a disdainful gesture the Arimathean counsellor,—'hath sought thy leave to lay it in his own new tomb with honour. Honour for a trickster and blasphemer!—If thou dost grant him this permit, I swear unto thee, Pilate, thou dost lend thyself unto a scheme of deep-laid cunning treachery!'

Still Pilate eyed him with the same fixed steadfastness.

'My centurion, thou sayest, is at fault'—he observed presently in cold meditative accents—'What centurion?'

'Petronius,—even he who was in charge. I made him accompany me hither. He waits without.'

'Call him, Justitia,'—said Pilate, seating himself upon his couch and assuming an attitude of ceremonious dignity and reserve.

Justitia obeyed, and in answer to her summons the centurion entered, saluted and stood silent.

'The "Nazarene" is dead?' said Pilate, addressing him in the measured tones of judicial inquiry.

'Sir, he hath been dead these two hours and more.'

'Thou art not herein deceived?'—and Pilate smiled strangely as he put the question.

Petronius stared in respectful amazement.

'My lord, we all beheld him die,—and one of us did pierce his side to hasten dissolution.'

'Why didst thou practise mercy thus?'

A troubled look clouded the soldier's honest face.

'Sir, there have been many terrors both in earth and air this day,—and—he seemed a sinless man and of a marvellous courage.'

Pilate turned towards Caiaphas. 'Seest thou the reason of this matter?' he said—'This Petronius is a Roman,—and 'tis in Roman blood to give some reverence to courage. Your Jew is no respecter of heroic virtues,—an' he were, he would not need to pay tribute unto Cæsar!'

The high-priest gave a scornful, half-derisive gesture.

'The very man now crucified, whose heroism thy soldier doth admire, was a Jew,'—he said.

'Not altogether,' interposed Joseph of Arimathea suddenly—'Mary, his mother, was of Egypt.'

Caiaphas sneered.

'And Joseph his father was of Nazareth,'—he said ; 'And as the father is, so is the son.'

At these words a singular silence fell upon the group. Justitia grew deadly pale, and leaned on the corner of her husband's couch for support, — her breath came and went hurriedly, and she laid one hand upon her bosom as though to still some teasing pain. Pilate half rose,—there was a strange light in his eyes, and he seemed about to speak,—but apparently on consideration altering his intention he sat down again, turning so wild a gaze upon Petronius that that officer was both dismayed and startled.

'Thou hast done well'—he said at last, breaking the oppressive stillness by an evident effort,—'Mercy doth well become a stalwart Roman, strong in brute strength as thou art. I blame thee not in aught! And thou, great Caiaphas'—here he fixed his eyes full on the high-priest, 'dost nobly practise sentiments which best befit thy calling,—revenge, bloodthirstiness and fear ! Peace!—snatch not the words from out my mouth by thy unseemly rage of interruption,

—I know the terror that thou hast of even the dead body of Him that thou hast slain,—but thou art too late in thy desire to carry cruelty beyond the grave. The Arimathean counsellor hath my permit to bury the "Nazarene" in honour even as he doth desire, in his own sepulchre newly hewn. But if thou dost suspect his good intent, and thinkest there is treachery in his honest service, seal thou the tomb thyself with thine own mark; and set a watch of as many as thou wilt, picked men and cautious, to guard the sepulchre till the third day be past. Thus shall all sides have justice, — thou, Joseph, and thou, Caiaphas, — and inasmuch as this Petronius showeth too much mercy, thou canst choose another centurion than he to head thy band. More I cannot do to satisfy demand '— here he broke off with a shuddering sigh of weariness.

' 'Tis enough '—said Caiaphas sullenly—' Nevertheless, Pilate, hadst thou been wise, thou would'st have refused the malefactor's body to this counsellor.'

And he darted an angry and suspicious glance at the Arimathean, who returned his look steadily.

' Hast urged enough against me, Caiaphas?' he

said—'Verily, were it not for my race and lineage, I
would take shame unto myself this day that I am
born a Jew, hearing thee vent such paltry rage and
puny fear, and thou the high-priest of the Temple!
But I will not bandy words with thee;—I do most
readily accept the judgment of our excellent lord the
governor, and herewith invite thee to be witness of
the burial of the "Nazarene." Thou canst examine
the sepulchre within and without to make thyself sure
there is no secret passage to serve for thy suspected
robbers of the dead. Bring thou thy seals of office,
and set a watch both night and day,—I give thee
promise that I will not hinder thee.'

Caiaphas bent his head in stiff and haughty acknowledgment, and turned on his heel to leave the
apartment, then glancing over his shoulder at the
pensive and drooping figure of Pilate, he said with
forced pleasantness,

'I wish thee better health, Pilate!'

'I thank thee, priest'—responded Pilate without
looking up—'I wish thee better courage!'

With an indifferent nod, Caiaphas was about to
leave the room, when, seeing that Petronius the

centurion had just saluted the governor and was also departing he stopped him by a gesture.

'Didst thou inquire as I bade thee, concerning young Iscariot?'

'Sir,' answered Petronius gravely—''tis rumoured in the city that Iscariot is dead.'

'Dead!' Caiaphas clutched at him to steady himself, for everything seemed suddenly reeling,—then he repeated again in a hoarse whisper—'Dead!'

For a moment the air around him grew black, and when he recovered his sickening senses, he saw that Pilate had risen and had come forward with his wife clinging to him, and that both were looking at him in undisguised astonishment, while Joseph of Arimathea was shaking him by the arm.

'What ails thee, Caiaphas?' asked the counsellor,—'Why art thou thus stricken suddenly?'

''Tis naught—'tis naught!' and the proud priest drew himself up erect, the while his eyes wandered to the face of the centurion once more,—'Thou didst say'—and he spoke with hesitation and difficulty—'that 'tis rumoured Judas is dead? Surely 'tis false,—how could he die?'

'Sir, he hath slain himself,—so runs the people's whisper.'

Caiaphas pressed one hand over his eyes to shut out the specks of red that swam before his sight like drops of blood. Then he looked round him with feigned composure—his countenance was very pale.

'See you!' he said unsteadily—'It can but move me to think that yesterday Judas was well and full of life, and that to-day he should be dead! A foolish youth,—of wild and erring impulse, but nevertheless much beloved by his father, and—his sister Judith'— Here he broke off with a fierce exclamation of mingled wrath and pain, and seizing the Arimathean by the arm, he cried boisterously—

'Come, thou subtle and righteous counsellor! On with me, and open thou thy rocky cave of death, that we may thrust within it the cause of all this mischief! Farewell, Pilate!—take health upon thee speedily and my blessing!—for thou hast done justice in this matter, albeit late, and forced from thee! And by thy legal sanction, I will set such a watch around the dead blasphemer's sepulchre as hath not been ex-celled in vigilance or guardianship for any treasure of the world!—his prophecy shall prove a lie! "After three days"! . . . nay!—not after a thousand and three! Let thunders crash, earth yawn, and mountains split asunder, the "Nazarene" shall never rise again!'

And with a wild gesture of defiance he rushed from the room, dragging the Arimathean with him, and followed by Petronius in a state of wonderment and fear.

XXVII

PILATE and his wife remained standing where they were for a moment, looking at each other in silence. The mingled light of the flickering lamps around them, and the moonbeams pouring in through the open window, gave a spectral pallor to their faces, which in absorbed expression reflected the same trouble; the same perplexed unquiet thought. After a pause, Pilate turned and moved feebly back to his couch,—Justitia following him.

'Oh, to escape this terror!' he murmured, as he sank among his pillows once more and closed his eyes—''Tis everywhere,—'tis upon Caiaphas, even as it is upon us all! A terror of the unknown, the un-declared, the invisible, the deathless! What hath been done this day we cannot comprehend,—we can but feel a mystery in the air,—and we grope blindly, seeing nothing — touching nothing — and therefore doubting everything, but nevertheless afraid! Afraid of what? Of ourselves? Nay, for we have killed the Man who did so much amaze us. What more then? Why, no more, since He is dead. And being dead, what cause is there for fear?'

He sighed heavily. Justitia knelt beside him.

'Dear my lord' — she began softly, her voice trembling a little. He turned his head towards her.

'What would'st thou say, Justitia?' he asked gently — 'Methinks my moods do trouble thee, thou most beloved of women, — I fain would be more cheerful for thy sake. But there is a darkness on my spirit that not even thy love can lift, — thou hast wept also, for I see the tears within thine eyes. Why art thou moved to weakness, thou strong heart? — what would they say of thee in Rome, thou who art adjudged a very queen of pride, if they beheld thee now?'

Justitia answered not, for all at once her head drooped upon her husband's breast, and clinging to him close, she gave way to a sudden paroxysm of passionate weeping. Pilate held her to him, soothing her with trembling touch and whispered words, now and again lifting his eyes to look with a kind of apprehension and expectancy round the silent room, as though he thought some one besides themselves witnessed their actions. After a while, when the violence of her sobbing ceased, he said—

'Tell me, Justitia—tell me all that troubles thee. Some secret grief thou hast kept pent up within thee through the day,—and what with storm and earth-quake, and darkness and thy fears for me, thou hast brooded on sorrow dumbly, as women often do when they have none to love them. But I who love thee more than life, Justitia, have the right to share thy heaviness,—I am strong enough, or should be strong, —look up!' and he raised her tearful face between his hands and gazed at her tenderly—'Unburden thy soul, Justitia! . . . tell me thy dream!'

With a cry she sprang erect, pushing back her ruffled hair from her brows, and gazing out into the moonlit garden with a strange expression of alarm and awe.

'No, no!' she whispered—'I cannot,—I dare not! 'Tis dark with the terror thou hast spoken of,—a

portent and a mystery; it brings no comfort,—and
thou canst not bear to hear more evil omens of
disaster'——

She broke off, adding presently in the same hushed
accents,

'Didst thou understand, Pontius, when Petronius
spoke, that Iscariot was dead?'

'Surely I understood'—responded Pilate—'What
marvel in it? 'Twas he that did betray his Master
to the priests. He dared not testify of this his
treachery,—and when I asked for him at this morning's trial, he could not be found. Out of remorse
he slew himself, or so I judge—a fitting death for
such a traitor. Thou dost not grieve for him?'

'I knew him not'—said Justitia thoughtfully—
'else — perchance if I had known — I might have
pitied him. But Judith loved him.'

Pilate moved impatiently among his cushions.

'Much do I marvel at thy interest in that most
haughty and most forward maiden'—he said—'That
she is beautiful I grant,—but vanity doth make her
beauty valueless. How camest thou to choose her
as a friend?'

'She is no friend of mine,' Justitia answered slowly, still looking out at the clear night—'Save that she hath been long left motherless, and is unguided and undisciplined, wherefore I have counselled her at times,—though truly my counsels are but wasted words, and she hath evil rooted in her soul. Nevertheless believe me, Pontius, now will her vanity have end,—for if she hath a heart, that heart will break to-night!'

Her husband made no reply, and a long silence fell between them. During this pause, a sound of joyous singing reached them,—a party of young men and maidens were strolling homeward from some festive meeting, thrumming on stringed instruments and carolling as they went. Over the wall of Pilate's enclosed garden their figures could be seen passing along the open street beyond, and occasional scraps of their conversation echoed distinctly through the air.

'Ephra, dost thou remember last week,' said a man's voice—'when the crowd went out to meet the "Nazarene" who died to-day? Canst recall the wild tune they sang? 'Twas passing sweet, and ended thus,—" Hosanna !"'

In a high pure tenor he sent the word pealing through the evening stillness,—his companions caught it up and chorussed all together

'Hosanna !—Hosanna !
Hosanna in the Highest !
Blessed is he that cometh,
That cometh in the name of the Lord !
Hosanna in the Highest ! '

The stirring triumph and grandeur of the melody seemed to terrify Justitia, for she caught at the heavy curtain that partially draped the window, and held it clenched in her hand convulsively as though for support, her whole frame trembling with some inward excitement. Suddenly the singing stopped, broken by laughter, and another voice cried out jestingly,—

' Beware the priests ! An' we raise such a chant as this, we shall all be crucified !'

They laughed again, and sauntering on, passed out of sight and hearing.

Justitia dropped the curtain from her grasp, and shivered as with deadly cold. Pilate watched her anxiously as she came slowly towards him step by step, and sat down on a low bench close to his couch, clasping her hands together in her lap and looking straight before her vaguely into empty air.

'Even so was the music in my dream'—she murmured—'Methought the very dead did rise and sing "Hosanna!"'

Pilate said nothing,—he seemed afraid to disturb the current of her thoughts. Presently raising her eyes to his, she asked—

'Dost thou in very truth desire to hear? Or will it weary thee?'

'Nay, it will comfort me,'—he answered, taking one of her listless hands and pressing it to his lips—'If any comfort I can have 'twill be in sharing whatever sorrow troubles thee. Speak on, and tell me all,—for from the very moment thou didst send to me this morning at the Tribunal, my soul has been perplexed with wondering at this act of thine,—so unlike thee at any time.'

Justitia sighed.

'Ay, it was unlike me,—and ever since, I have been most unlike myself. Thou knowest 'twas a morning dream,—for night was past, and thou hadst

but lately left me to take thy place within the Hall
of Judgment. I had arisen from my bed,—but as
yet I had not called my women, and partially arrayed,
I sat before my mirror, slowly binding up my hair.
My eyes were strangely heavy and my thoughts
confused, — and suddenly the polished surface of
the metal into which I gazed, grew black, even
as a clear sky darkening with storm. Then came
a noise as of many waters thundering in my ears,
—and after that I know not what did chance to
me. Nevertheless it seemed I was awake, and
wandering solitary within some quiet region of
eternal shade.'

She paused, trembling a little, then went on—

'A solemn depth of peace it seemed to be, wherein
was neither landscape, light nor air. Methought I
stood upon a rift of rock gazing far downward,—
and there before mine eyes were laid millions on
millions of the dead,—dead men and women white
as parchment or bleached bone. Side by side in
wondrous state they lay,—and over them all brooded
a pale shadow as of outspread wings. And as I
looked upon them all and marvelled at their endless

numbers, a rush of music sounded like great harps
swung in the wind, and far away a Voice thundered
"*Hosanna!*" And lo!—the pale shadow of wings
above the dead, furled up and vanished, and
through some unseen portal came a blazing Cross
of Light, and after it, white as a summer cloud
and glorious as the sun, followed—the "Nazarene"!
"Awake, ye dead!" He cried—"Awake, for Death
is ended! Awake and pass from hence to Life!"
And they awoke!—yea, they awoke in all the pleni-
tude of strength and wondrous beauty, those millions
upon millions of long-perished mortals,—they uprose
in radiant ranks, like flowers breaking into bloom,—
adorned with rays of light they stood, great angels
every one, and cried aloud—"Glory to thee, O
Christ, thou Messenger of God! Glory to thee,
thou holy Pardoner of our sins! Thou Giver of
Eternal Life! Glory to thee, Redeemer of the
world! we praise and worship thee for ever!" Then
was my dreaming spirit seized with shuddering and
fear,—I turned away mine eyes, unable to endure
the dazzling luminance and wonder,—and when I
looked again, the scene was changed.'

Here Justitia broke off, and leaning closer to her husband, caught both his hands in hers, and gazed earnestly into his face.

'Thinkest thou not,' she whispered—'that this vision was strange? Why should it come to me?— I who ever doubted all gods, and have in my soul accepted death as each man's final end? 'Tis a thought most unwelcome to me,—that the dead should rise!'

Pilate met her eyes with a wistful woe and sympathy in his own.

'Yea, 'tis unwelcome'—he said—'I would not live again had I the choice. For we do things in this our life 'twere best not to remember,—and having sinned, one's only rescue is to die,—die utterly and so forget we ever were. Yet perchance there is no forgetfulness,— there may be an eternal part within us,'—he stopped, gazing around him nervously— 'Hast thou no more to tell?—this was not all thy dream?'

'Ah no!' cried Justitia, rising from her seat with an unconscious gesture of desperation—'Would that it were! For what remains is naught but horror,—

horror and mystery and pain! 'Tis what I further saw within my vision that made me send my message in such haste to thee,—I thought I might avert misfortune and ward off evil from thy path, my husband, for if dreams have any truth, which I pray they have not, thou art surely threatened with some nameless doom!'

Pilate looked up at her troubled face, and smiled forcedly.

'Fear not for me, Justitia'—he said—'Trust me there is no other doom save death, and that doth hourly threaten every man. I marvel at thy tremors, —thou who art wontedly of so bold a spirit! Rally thy usual courage!—surely I shall not die of hearing of disaster in a dream! Speak on!—what else didst thou behold?'

'I beheld a mighty ocean'—replied Justitia, raising one hand solemnly as she spoke—'And this ocean was of human blood and covered all the earth! And methought every drop within that scarlet sea did have a voice of mingled tears and triumph, that cried aloud "Hail, Jesus of Nazareth, Son of the God Eternal!" Then on the ghastly waves there floated, even as floats a ship, a wondrous temple, gleaming with gold and precious stones, and on the summit of its loftiest pinnacle a jewelled Cross did shine. And in my dream I understood that all the kings and emperors and counsellors of the world had reared this stately fabric to the memory and the worship of the "Nazarene"!'

'To the memory and the worship of the "Nazarene"!' repeated Pilate slowly—'A temple floating on a sea of blood!—well,—what then?'

'Then,' went on Justitia, her dark eyes dilating as she grew more and more absorbed in her narration—'then I saw the heavens rent asunder, and many wondrous faces, beautiful and wise, but sorrowful, looked down. And from the waves of blood arose wild sounds of lamentation and despair, and as I listened I comprehended that the lofty floating temple I beheld was crushing underneath it the struggling souls of men. "How long, O Lord! how long!" they cried, and "Save, Lord, or we perish!" Then came a great and terrible noise as of martial music mixed with thunder, and lo! a mighty Sword fell straight from Heaven, and smote the temple in the midst so that it parted in twain, and drifted on the crimson flood a wreck,—and even as it split, I saw the secret of its wickedness,—an altar splashed with blood and strewn with dead men's bones, and over-flowing in every part with bags of gold ill-gotten,—and fronting it in lewdest mockery of worship, with lies upon his lips and coin grasped in both his hands, there knelt a leering Devil in a Priest's disguise!'

She paused, breathing quickly in a kind of suppressed excitement—then continued,

'Now, as I watched the sundered halves of the smitten temple, drifting to right and left, and circling round about to sink, a wrathful voice exclaimed, "*Many shall call upon Me, saying, Lord, Lord, have we not prophesied in thy name, and in thy name done many wonderful works? And I will say unto them—Depart from Me, I never knew ye, ye workers of iniquity!*" And even as the Voice sounded, the temple sank ; and naught was left of it but the topmost Cross, floating alone upon the sea!'

'Always the Cross!' murmured Pilate perplexedly ; 'Doth it threaten to become a symbol?'

'I know not,' answered Justitia with a far-off dreamy expression in her face—'nevertheless 'twas ever present in my dream. And now to hear the end,—methought I watched the lonely Cross tossed by itself upon the sea, and wondered whether, like the temple it had once adorned, 'twould also sink. To and fro it floated, shining like a star, and presently I saw that wherever it rested for a space, it changed the waves of blood to a light like liquid fire. Then happened a strange marvel;—out of the far distance came a ship, sailing straightly and with speed,—'twas small and light and white as foam, and within it, steering boldly onward, sat a woman alone. And as her vessel sped across the dreadful sea, great monsters of the deep arose and threatened her,—the pallid hands of drowned men clutched at her,—noises there were of earthquake and of thunder,—nevertheless she sailed on fearlessly, and as she journeyed, smiled and sang. And I beheld her course with wonderment, for she was steering steadily towards the Cross that floated lost upon the waves. Nearer she came, and soon she reached it, and leaning from her vessel's edge, she caught it in both hands and raised it up

towards heaven. "Jesus, thou Messenger of God!"
she cried—"Through thy great Love we claim eternal
Glory!" And with the swiftness of lightning she
was answered!—the sea of blood was changed to
living flame,—her ship became a cloud of light, and
she herself an angel clad in wings, and from the Cross
she held streamed such a splendour as illumined all
the heavens! And with thunder and with music
and rejoicing, the gateways of the air, methought,
were opened, and with a thousand thousand winged
creatures round Him and above Him, and a new
world rising like the morning sun behind Him, again,
again I saw—the "Nazarene"! And with a voice of
silver-sweet and overwhelming triumph He proclaimed: "*Heaven and earth shall pass away, but My
words shall not pass away!*"'

She waited a moment, then went on—

'The "Nazarene"!—no other than the "Nazarene" it
was whom I beheld thus gloriously surrounded!—
the very "Nazarene" whom thou, Pontius, wert asked
to judge and to condemn! No marvel was it that
I sent to thee,—and in my scroll I would have told
thee I had dreamt He was a god, but that I feared

some other eye than thine might intercept and scan my words. Therefore I wrote "have naught to do with that just man,"—alas! 'twas foolish of me!— thou could'st not listen to a woman's pleading in a matter of the law, and when my slave returned I knew mine errand had been fruitless. Nevertheless I strove to warn thee '——

'Of what?' asked Pilate hoarsely,—he had covered his eyes with his hand, and spoke with difficulty— 'Of naught, save that being just 'twere pity He should die. But knowest thou not 'tis ever the just who are condemned? And that thou didst suffer in a dream was better than my case;—what I saw, and what I suffered, was no dream!'

He sighed bitterly, heavily, and Justitia sitting down beside him, leaned her head upon his shoulder.

'I have not yet told thee all;'—she said in a trembling voice,—'The rest concerns thy fate!'

Pilate removed his hand from his eyes and looked round at her.

'My fate!' he echoed indifferently—'Whate'er it be, surely I shall have force enough to meet it!'

She held his hands in both her own and pressed them convulsively.

'Ay, full well I know thou hast force enough for anything'—she said—'else thou would'st not be Roman. But to perish even as Iscariot'——

He started away from her.

'As Iscariot!' he cried indignantly—'Nay, I am no traitor!'

She looked at him, her face growing very white and her lips trembling. She was evidently nerving herself to utter something which she feared would be unwelcome.

'The gods might call thee coward, Pontius!' she said at last faintly, and as though the words were wrested out of her.

He turned upon her in astonishment and wrath.

'What didst thou say, Justitia?' he demanded fiercely—'Surely I have not heard thee aright?— thou didst not dare speak such a word to me as "coward"?'

Her heart beat violently, but she kept her eyes fixed upon him tenderly, and without any visible sign of fear.

' If thou didst see supernal glory in the " Nazarene " '
—she faltered slowly, and then paused, leaving her
sentence unfinished.

Pilate's head drooped,—he shrank and shivered as
though some invisible hand had struck him with a
heavy blow.

'Go on,' he said unsteadily—'Albeit I know,—I
know now what thou would'st say.'

' If thou didst see supernal glory in the "Nazarene,"'
she repeated in firmer accents—' if thou didst recognise
the God behind the Man, ay, even to swoon thereat,
surely thou should'st have openly proclaimed this
truth unto the priests and people.'

' They would not have believed me '—he answered
her in a husky whisper,—' They would have deemed
me mad,—unfit to rule '——

'What matter?' said Justitia dauntlessly,—'What
are the beliefs of priests or people measured against
the utterance of a Truth? If thou hadst spoken '——

' I tell thee they would have called me crazed '—
said Pilate, rising and pacing the room agitatedly—
'They would have told me that my vision was
deceived,—that my brain wandered. How could'st

thou ever persuade a callous crowd, of the existence
of the supernatural?'

'How do they persuade themselves?' demanded
Justitia—'These very Jews do swear by supernatural
shows that seem impossible. Do they not say that
God Himself taught Moses the Commandments on
Mount Sinai?—will they not even accept as truth
that their most vengeful Jehovah hath oft condoned
murder as a holy sacrifice, as in the story of their
own judge Jephthah, who slew his innocent daughter
to satisfy the horrible bloodthirstiness of Heaven!
Why should the supernatural seem less to be believed
in one phase of existence than another?'

'I know not—I know not!'—answered Pilate still
walking to and fro distressfully,—'Make me not
answerable for the inconsistencies of man! I did my
best and utmost with the people,—if I had told them
what I saw, they would have dragged me from the judg-
ment-seat as one possessed of devils and distraught;
and Cæsar would have stripped me of authority.'

'Thou could'st have suffered all loss with equa-
nimity,' said Justitia thoughtfully—'provided thine
own conscience had been clear.'

He gave her no response, but still paced restlessly up and down.

Justitia moved to the window and gazed out at the dark, smooth velvet-looking foliage of the fig-trees at the end of the garden.

'It was a pale bright light, even like the beaming of this very moon'—she said—'that shone upon me in the closing of my dream. I stood, methought, in one of the strangest, loneliest, wildest corners of the world,—great mountain-peaks towered around me, white and sparkling with a seeming-bitter cold, and at my feet a solemn pool lay black and stirless. And as I looked, I saw thee, Pontius!—I saw thee flitting even as a spectre among the jagged rocks of those most solitary hills,—thou wert old and wan and weary, and hadst the livid paleness of approaching death. I called thee, but thou would'st not answer,— onward thou didst tread, and cam'st so near to me I could have touched thee! but ever thou didst elude my grasp. All suddenly'—and here she turned towards her husband, her eyes darkening with her thoughts—'I beheld thee, drifting like a cloud blown by the wind, towards a jutting peak that bent above

that dreary pool of waveless waters—there thou didst
pause, and with a cry that pierced my soul, thou
didst exclaim "Jesus of Nazareth, thou Son of God,
have mercy on me!" Then,—ere I could bid thee
turn and wait for me, thou didst plunge forward,—
forward and down,—down into the chill and darksome
lake which closed even as a grave above thee!—thou
wert gone,—gone into death and silence,—and I,
shrieking upon thy name, awoke!'

'And waking thus in terror thou didst send to
me?' asked Pilate gently, approaching her where she
stood, and encircling her with his arm.

She bent her head in assent.

'Even then. And later, when my messenger
returned from thee, I heard the people shout "*Not
this man, but Barabbas.*" Who is Barabbas?'

'A thief and murderer'—said Pilate quickly—'But
he hath the popular sympathy. Once he was in the
honourable employ of Shadeen, the Persian jewel-
merchant of this city,—and as a reward for trust
reposed in him, he stole some priceless pearls from
out a private coffer of his master. Moreover he was
one of a band of revolutionary malcontents, and did

stab to death the Pharisee Gabrias, out in the open streets. 'Tis more than eighteen months ago now— thou wert visiting thy friends in Rome, and knewest naught of it. I would have had Barabbas crucified,— nevertheless the people have given him rescue and full liberty. They celebrate their feast by the release of a murderer, and the slaughter of the Sinless. 'Tis their chosen way—and I am not to blame!'

'Iscariot also served in the house of Shadeen,' said Justitia meditatively.

'Even so I have heard.'

'And thou art not troubled, Pontius, by my dream?' she questioned earnestly—'Seest thou no omen in its end concerning thee, when I beheld thee perish in the gloom and solitude, self-slain, even as Iscariot?'

He shuddered a little and forced a faint smile.

'If I am troubled, Justitia, 'tis because thou art,— and because trouble doth vaguely press upon us all to-day. Trust me, the very Jews are not without their fears, seeing that the storm hath rent their Temple veil, and darkened the land with such mysterious suddenness. 'Tis enough to shake the spirits of the boldest,—but now perchance evil is past, and by and by the air will rid itself of all forebodings. Lo, how divinely clear the sky!—how fair the moon!—'tis a silver night for the slumber of the "Nazarene"!'

She looked at him with wondering, dilating eyes.

'Speakest thou in sober reason, Pontius?' she said 'Wilt thou insist upon thy fancy that He is not dead, and that He cannot die? Thinkest thou He only sleeps?'

Pilate drew her closer to him.

'Hush,—hush!' he said in a low trembling tone—'Whatever I may think, I must say nothing. Let us hold our peace,—let us live as the world would have us live, in the proud assumption that there is nothing in the universe more powerful or more wonderful than ourselves! So shall we fit ourselves for the material side of nature,—and if there be in truth, another side,—a spiritual, we can shut our eyes and swear we know naught of it! So shall we be deemed wise,—and sane!—and we shall give offence to no one —save to God,—if a God perchance there be!'

His voice grew faint—his eyes had a vacant stare,
—he was looking out and upward to the brilliant
sky. Suddenly he brought his gaze down from the
heavens to earth, and fixed it on the open road beyond
his garden where a small dark group of slowly
moving figures just then appeared.

'Who goes yonder?' he said inquiringly—'Seest
thou, Justitia, they take the private path towards the
house of Iscariot? Surely they carry some heavy
burden?'

Justitia leaned forward to look,—then drew back
with a faint cry.

'Come away,—come away!' she whispered, shiver-
ing and drawing her flowing robes closer about her—
'Do not wait here—do not watch them,—they are
bearing home the dead!'

'The dead!' echoed Pilate—'Then 'tis the body of
Judas!'

Justitia laid her hand entreatingly against his
lips.

'Hush—hush! If it be, as indeed I feel it is, do
not speak of it—do not look!'—And with agitated
impatience she drew the curtain across the window

and shut out the solemn beauty of the night—' I am chilled with horror, Pontius,—I can bear no more ! I would not see dead Judas in my dreams ! Let us go hence and rest, and try to sleep, and,—if we can,— forget ! '

XXVIII

THAT same night, before a richly-chased mirror of purely polished silver, and gazing at her own fair face reflected in it by the brilliant lustre of the moon, Judith Iscariot sat, lost in a pleasant reverie. She was alone, — she had dismissed her attendant women,—the picture of her perfect loveliness, rendered lovelier by the softness of the lunar beams, charmed her, and she would not have so much as a small hand-lamp kindled, lest its wavering flicker should destroy the magical effect of her beauty mirrored thus and set about with glory by the argent light of heaven. Leaning back in a low carved chair, she clasped her round arms idly behind her head and contemplated herself critically with a smile. She had cast aside the bright flame-tinted mantle she had worn all day, and was now arrayed in white,—a

straight plain robe of thin and silky texture that clung
about her figure closely, betraying every exquisite
curve and graceful line,—her fiery-golden hair un-
bound to its full length fell to the very floor in
glistening showers, and from underneath the thick
bright ripples of it clustering on her brow, her dark
jewel-like eyes flashed with a mingling of joy and
scorn.

'What cowards, after all, are men!' she murmured
half aloud,—'Even the strongest! Yon base Barabbas
was nigh to weeping for the death of the accursëd
"Nazarene,"—methinks 'twas terror for himself, rather
than pity for the dying. And Caiaphas!—who
would have thought that he would be paralysed with
fear when they told him of the rending of the Temple
veil!'

She laughed softly,—and her lips laughing back at
her from the silver surface into which she gazed, had
so bewitching a sweetness in their smile that she
leaned forward to observe them more intently.

'Verily 'tis no marvel that they dote upon me one
and all'—she said, studying her delicate features and
dazzling complexion with complacent vanity,—'Even

smiling so, I draw the subtle Caiaphas my way,—he
passeth for a wise priest, yet if I do but set my eyes
upon him thus '—and she half closed them and peered
languorously through their sweeping lashes—' he pales
and trembles,—or thus '—and she flashed them fully
open in all their fatal brilliancy—' he loses breath for
very love, and gapes upon me, flushed and foolish like
one stricken with the burning of the sun.   And
Barabbas,—I must rid me of Barabbas, though there
is something fierce about him that I love; albeit he
showed but little love for me to-day, shaken and
palsied as he was by cowardice.'

She took up a comb and began to pass it slowly
through the shining splendour of her hair.   Gradually
her face became more meditative, and a slight frown
contracted her brows.

'Nevertheless there was a horror in that storm!'—
she continued in whispered accents—' And even now
my heart misgives me strangely,—I would that Judas
were at home!'

She rose up, slim and stately, and stood before her
mirror, the golden weight of half her tresses in one
hand.   Round about her the moonlight fell in a

glistening halo, touching here and there a jewel on her arm or bosom to a sudden glimmer of white fire.

'Caiaphas should have told the people what I bade him '—she murmured, 'that the tempest was awakened by the evil sorceries of the "Nazarene." He was possessed of devils; and they did cause the pitchy darkness and the tremor of the earth that rent the rocks asunder. 'Twas even so,—and Caiaphas should have spoken thus,—but he too, for the moment, lost judgment through his fears.'

Pausing, she twisted her hair mechanically round and round her fingers.

'What was the magic of the Man of Nazareth?' she queried, as though making the inquiry of her own reflection that gazed earnestly back at her from the silver oval surface she confronted—'I could see none save beauty. Beauty He had undoubtedly,—but not such beauty as a woman loves. 'Twas too austere and perfect,—too grave and passionless,—albeit He had strange light within His eyes that for a passing second moved me, even me, to terror! And then the thunder came,—and then the darkness '——

She shivered slightly, then laughed, and glanced up at the moon that shone, round and full, in at her open casement.

''Twas a malignant spell He cast,' she said—'But now 'tis ended,—and all alarms have ceased. And truly it is well for us that He is dead, for such fanatics are dangerous. And now is Judas undeceived,—he knows this prophet whom he called his Master is no god after all, but simply man,—and he will repent him of his wanderings and return to us again. When his first rage is past, he will come back ashamed and sorrowful, and seeking pardon for his fury of last night,—and we will welcome him with joy and feasting and forgiveness, and once more we shall be happy. Yea, surely Caiaphas did advise me well, and in the death of the blasphemous " Nazarene " Judas is saved from further harm.'

She threw back her hair over her shoulders and smiled. Then opening a massive brass-bound casket near her, she drew forth a handful of various jewels, and looked at them carelessly one by one, selecting at last a star-shaped ornament of magnificent rubies.

''Tis a fair gift'—she murmured, holding it up in

the moonlight and watching it flash a dull red in the silver rays—' I know not that I have ever seen a fairer ! 'Twas wise of Caiaphas not to bestow this on his sickly spouse,—'twould ill become the pallid skin of the daughter of Annas.'

She studied the gems carefully,—then diving anew into the casket brought out a chain of exquisite pearls, each pearl as large as the ripe seed of Indian maize.

'How well they go together thus!' she said, setting them with the ruby star against the whiteness of her bare arm—'They should be worn in company,—the high-priest's rubies and the stolen pearls of Barabbas!'

Her lips parted in a little mocking smile, and for a moment or two she held the gems in her hand, absorbed in thought. Then, slowly fastening the pearls round her throat, she put back the ruby pendant into the jewel-coffer, and again peered at herself in the silver mirror. And as she silently absorbed the glowing radiance of her own matchless beauty, she raised her arms with a gesture of irrepressible triumph.

'For such as I am, the world is made!' she exclaimed — 'For such as I am, emperors and kings

madden themselves and die! For such as I am,
proud heroes abase themselves as slaves. No
woman lives who can be fairer than I,—and what
shall I do with my fairness when I am weary of
sporting with lovers and fools?—I will wed some
mighty conqueror, and be the queen and mistress
of many nations!'

In her superb vanity, she lifted her head higher as
though she felt the imagined crown already on her
brows, and stepped slowly backward from the mirror,
still steadfastly regarding her own image, when all
at once the sound of a hurried footfall in the corridor
startled her. She turned in a listening attitude, her
hair falling about her, and the pearls gleaming on
her throat,—the hasty footstep came nearer,—then
paused.

'Madam! Madam!' cried a voice outside.

Moved by some swift instinct of alarm, she sprang
forward and flung the door of her chamber wide
open, thus confronting one of her father's servants,
who stared at her wildly, making dumb signs of
despair.

'What is it?' she gasped,—her lips had grown

suddenly stiff and dry and she could barely articulate, —her heart beat violently, and the pearls about her neck seemed strangling her.

The man opened his mouth to answer, then stopped,—Judith clutched him by the arm.

'Speak!'—she whispered—'What evil news hast thou?'

'Madam,' faltered the servant, trembling—'I dare not utter it,—prithee come—thy father sends—have patience . . . take comfort'——

He turned from her, hiding his face.

''Tis Judas!' she exclaimed—'He is wounded?— ill? He hath returned?'

'Ay, madam, he hath returned!' replied the messenger hoarsely, and then, as if fearing to trust himself to the utterance of another word, he hastened away, mutely entreating her to follow.

She paused a moment, — a ghastly pallor stole away all the light and brilliancy of her features, and she pressed one hand upon her bosom to control its rising fear.

'He hath returned!' she murmured vaguely— 'Judas is at home! My father sends for me?—then all is well,—surely 'tis well,—it cannot be otherwise than well.'

Giving one glance backward into her moonlit room where the silver mirror shone like a glistening shield, she began to move with hesitating step through the corridor, — then, all at once seized by an irresistible panic, she gathered up her trailing white robes in her hand and ran precipitately towards the great vestibule of the house, which her father had had built in the fashion of an Egyptian court, and where he was accustomed to sit in the cool of the evening with his intimates and friends. It was surrounded with square columns and was open to the night, and as Judith came rushing along, her gold hair flying about her like flame, and her dark eyes wild with uncertain terror and expectancy, she was confronted by the tall figure of a man who, with extended arms, strove to intercept himself between her and some passive object that lay, covered with a cloth, on the ground a few steps beyond. She gazed at him amazedly,—it was Barabbas.

'Judith!' he faltered — 'Judith, — wait! — Have patience'——

But she pushed him aside, and ran towards her
father, whom she perceived leaning against one of
the carven columns, his face hidden upon his arm.

'Father!' she cried.

He raised his head and looked at her,—his austere
fine features were convulsed by a speechless agony
of grief, and with one trembling hand he pointed
silently to the stirless covered shape that reposed at
a little distance from him. Her eyes followed his
gesture, and, staggering forward feebly step by step,
she pushed back her hair from her brows and stared
fixedly at the outline of the thing that was so
solemnly inert. Then the full comprehension of
what she saw seemed to burst in upon her brain,
and falling upon her knees she clutched desperately
at the rough cloth which concealed that which she
craved, yet feared to see.

'Judas!' she cried—'Judas!'

Her voice broke in a sharp shriek, and she suddenly withdrew her hands and looked at them in
horror, shuddering, as though they had come in
contact with some nameless abomination. Lifting
her eyes she became dimly conscious that others

were around her,—that her father had approached,
—that Barabbas was gazing at her,—and with a
bewildered vacant smile she pointed to the hidden
dead.

'Why have ye brought him home thus wrapped
from light and air?' she demanded in quick jarring
accents—'It may be that he sleeps,—or hath swooned.
Uncover his face!'

No one moved to obey her. The veiled corpse
lying black and stirless in the full light of the moon
had something solemnly forbidding in its aspect.
And for one or two minutes a profound and awful
stillness reigned, unbroken save by the slow chime of
a bell striking the midnight hour.

Suddenly Judith's voice began again, murmuring
in rapid whispers.

'Judas,—Judas!' she said, 'waken! 'Tis folly to
lie there and fill me with such terrors,—thou art not
dead,—it is not possible,—thou could'st not die thus
suddenly. Only last night thou camest here full of
a foolish rage against me, and in thy thoughtless
frenzy thou didst curse me,—lo, now thou must
unsay that curse,—thou canst not leave me un-

forgiven and unblessed. What have I ever done of
harm to thee? I did but bid thee prove the treachery
of the "Nazarene." And thou hast proved it; wherefore should'st thou grieve to find deception at an end?
Rise up, rise up!—if thou art ill 'tis I will tend thee,
—waken!—why should'st thou rest sullen thus, and
angry still? Surely 'tis I who should be angry at
thy churlishness, for well I know thou hear'st my
voice, though out of some sick humour, as it seems,
thou wilt not answer me!'

And once more her hands hovered hesitatingly in
the air, till apparently nerving herself to a supreme
effort, she took trembling hold of the upper part of
the pall-like drapery that hid the corpse from view.
Lifting it fearfully, she turned it back, slowly, slowly,
—then stared in horrid wonderment,—was that her
brother's face she looked upon?—that fair, strange,
pallid marble mask with those protruding desperate
eyes? Such fixed impenetrable eyes!—they gave
her wondering stare for stare,—and as she stooped
down close, and closer yet, her warm red lips went
nigh to touch those livid purple ones, which were
drawn back tightly just above the teeth in the ghastly

semblance of a smile. She stroked the damp and
ice-cold brow,—she thrust her fingers in the wild hair,
—it was most truly Judas, or some dreadful likeness
of him that lay there in waxen effigy,—a white and
frozen figure of dead youth and beauty,—and yet she
could not realise the awful truth of what she saw.
Suddenly her wandering and distrustful gaze fell on
his throat,—a rope was round it, twisted in such
a knot, that where it pressed the flesh the skin was
broken, and the bruised blood, oozing through, had
dried and made a clotted crimson mark as though
some jagged knife had hacked it. Beholding this,
she leapt erect, and tossing her arms distractedly
above her head, gave vent to a piercing scream that
drove sharp discord through the air, and brought the
servants of the household running in with torches in
the wildest confusion and alarm. Her father caught
her in his arms, endeavouring to hold and pacify her,
—in vain!—he might as well have striven to repress
a whirlwind. She was transformed into a living
breathing fury, and writhed and twisted in his grasp,
a convulsed figure of heartrending despair.

‘Look you, they have murdered him!’ she shrieked;

'They have murdered Judas! — he hath been violently slain by the followers of the "Nazarene"! O cruel deed!—There shall be vengeance for it,— vengeance deep and bitter,—for Judas had no fault at all save that of honesty! Caiaphas! Caiaphas! Where is Caiaphas? Bid him come hither and behold this work!—bid him pursue and crucify the murderers!—let us go seek the Roman governor,— justice, I say!—I will have justice'— Here her shrill voice suddenly sank, and flinging herself desperately across her brother's body, she tried with shaking fingers to loosen the terrible death-noose of the strangling cord.

'Undo this knot'—she cried sobbingly—'O God! will none of ye remove this pressure that doth stop his breath? Maybe he lives yet!—his eyes have sense and memory in them,—untie this twisted torture, — prithee help me, friends, — father, help me'——

Even as she spoke, with her fingers plucking at the cord, an awful change passed over her face, and snatching her hands away she looked at them aghast, —they were wet with blood. A strange light kindled in her eyes,—a wan smile hovered on her lips. She held up her stained fingers.

'Lo, he bleeds!' she said—'The life within him rises to my touch,—he is not dead!'

'He bleeds as dead men oft are wont to bleed at the touch of their murderers!'—said a harsh voice suddenly,—'Thou, Judith, hast brought thy brother to his death,—wherefore his very blood accuses thee!'

And the rugged figure of Peter, advancing, stood out clear in the moonbeams that fell showering on the open court.

Iscariot, tall and stately, confronted him in wrath and astonishment.

'Man, how darest thou at such a time thus rave upon my daughter'— he began, then stopped, checked in his speech by the austere dignity of the disciple's attitude and his regal, half-menacing gesture.

'Back, Jew!' he said—'Thou who art not born again of water or of spirit, but art ever of the tainted blood of Israel unregenerate, contest no words with me! Remorse hath made me strong! I am that Peter who denied his Master, and out of sin repented of, I snatch authority! Dispute me not,—I speak

not unto thee, but unto her;—she who doth clamour
for swift justice on the murderers of her brother there.
Even so do *I* cry out for justice!—even so do *I*
demand vengeance!—vengeance upon her who drove
him to his doom. For Judas was my friend,—and by
his own hand was he slain,—but in that desperate
deed no soul took part save she who now bemoans
the end that hath been wrought, through the tempt-
ing of her serpent subtilty!'

'Hast thou no mercy?' cried Barabbas in an
agony, ' Not even at this hour?'

'Not at this hour nor at any hour!' responded
Peter with fierce triumph lighting up his features,—
'God forbid that I should show any mercy to the
wicked!'

'There spoke the first purely human Christian!'
murmured a low satirical voice, and the picturesque
form of Melchior shadowed itself against a marble
column whitened by the moon—'Verily, Petrus, thou
shalt convey to men in a new form the message of
Love Divine!'

But the disciple heeded not these words. He strode
forward to where Judith lay half prone across her

brother's corpse, still busying herself with efforts to untie the suicidal noose at the throat, which was now darkly moist with blood.

'What doest thou there, Judith Iscariot?' he demanded—'Thou canst never unfasten that hempen necklet,—'tis not of pearls or sparkling gems such as thy soul loveth,—and Judas himself hath knotted it too closely for easy severance. Let be, let be,—weep and lament for thine own treachery,—for behold a curse shall fall upon thee, never to be lifted from thy life again!'

She heard,—and raising her eyes, which were dry and glittering with fever, smiled at him. So wildly beautiful did she look, that Peter, though wrought up to an exaltation of wrath, was for a moment staggered by the bewildering loveliness of her perfect face showered round by its wealth of red-gold hair, and hesitated to pronounce the malediction that hovered on his lips.

'Never again, — never again' — she murmured vaguely; 'See!' And she showed him her blood-stained fingers—'Life lingers in him yet!—ah, prithee, friend,' —and she gazed up at him appealingly—'Undo the

cruel cord!—if Judas tied it, . . . didst thou not tell
me Judas tied it? . . . how could that be?'— She
paused,—a puzzled look knitting her brows,—then a
sudden terror began to shake her limbs.

'Father!' she exclaimed.

He hastened to her, and lifting her up, pressed
her against his breast, the tears raining down his
face.

'What does it mean?' she faltered, gazing at him
alarmedly—'Tell me,—it is not true, . . . it cannot
be true,—Judas was ever brave and bold,—he did not
wreak this violence upon himself?'

Iscariot strove to answer her, but words failed him,
—the wonted calmness of his austerely handsome
features was completely broken up by misery and
agitation. She however, gazing fully at him, understood at last,—and, wrenching herself out of his arms,
stood for a moment immovable and ghastly pale, as
though suddenly turned to stone. Then, lifting her
incarnadined hands in the bright moon-rays, she broke
into a discordant peal of delirious laughter.

'O terrible Nazarene!' she cried—'This is thy
work! Thy sorceries have triumphed!—thou hast

thy victory! Thou art avenged in full, thou pitiless, treacherous Nazarene!'

And with a sharp shriek that seemed to stab the stillness with a wound, she fell forward on the pavement in a swoon; as lost to sense and sight as the body of Judas, that with its fixed wide-open eyes, stared blindly outward into nothingness and smiled.

XXIX

THEY carried her to her own chamber and left
her to the ministrations of her women, who
wept for her as women will often weep when
startled by the news of some tragic event which
does not personally concern them, without feeling
any real sympathy with the actual cause of
sorrow. Her haughty and arrogant disposition had
made her but few friends among her own sex, and
her peerless beauty had ever been a source of ill-
will and envy to others less dazzlingly fair. So
that the very maidens who tended her in her
fallen pride and bitter heart break, though they
shed tears for pure nervousness, had little love
in their enforced care, and watched her in her
deep swoon with but casual interest, only whisper-

ing vague guesses one to another as to what
would be her possible condition when she again
awoke to consciousness.

Meanwhile her brother's corpse was reverently
placed on two carved and gilded trestles set in
an arched recess of the open court, and draped
with broideries of violet and gold. In stern
silence and constrained composure, the unhappy
father of the dead man gave his formal instruc-
tions, and fulfilled in every trifling particular the
duties that devolved upon him, — and when all
had been done that was demanded of him for
the immediate moment, he turned towards those
three who had brought home the body of his
son between them, — Barabbas, Melchior, and the
disciple Peter.

'Sirs,' he said in a low voice broken by emotion—'I have to thank ye for the sorrowful service
ye have rendered me,—albeit it hath broken my
heart and hath visited upon our house such
mourning as shall never cease. Only one of ye
am I in any sort acquainted with, — and that
is Barabbas, lately the prisoner of the law. In

former days he hath been welcomed here, and
deemed a worthy man and true, and now, despite
his well-proved crimes and shame of punishment, I
can but bear in mind that once he was my
son's companion in the house of El - Shadeen.'
Here his accents faltered, but he controlled himself
and went on—'Wherefore, excusing not his faults,
I yet would say that even as the people have released
him, I cannot visit him with censure, inasmuch as he
hath evident pity for my grief, and did appeal for
my beloved child against the mercilessness of this
stranger.'

Pausing, he turned his eyes upon Peter, who met
his gaze boldly.

'Stranger I truly am from henceforth to the Jews,'
said the disciple,—'Naught have I in common with
their lives, spent in the filthy worship of Mammon
and the ways of usury. Nevertheless I compassionate
thy fate, Iscariot, as I compassionate the fate of any
wretched man stricken with woes innumerable through
his own blindness and unbelief ;—and as for mercilessness, whereof thou dost accuse me, thou shalt find
the Truth ever as a sword inclement, sharp to cut

away all pleasingly delusive forms. When thou dost speak of thy beloved child, thou dost betray the weakness of thy life, for from thy nest of over-pampering and indulgent love hath risen a poison snake to sting and slay! A woman left unguarded and without authority upon her, is even as a devil that destroys, — a virgin given liberty of will is soon deflowered. Knowest thou not thy Judith is a wanton?—and that thy ravening high-priest Caiaphas hath made of her a viler thing than ever was the city's Magdalen? Ah, strike an' thou wilt, Iscariot!—the truth is on my lips!—tear out my tongue, and thou shalt find the truth still there!'

Speechless with wrath, Iscariot made one fierce stride towards him with full intent to smite him across the mouth as the only fitting answer to his accusation, but as he raised his threatening hand, the straight unquailing look of the now almost infuriate disciple, struck him with a sudden supernatural awe, and he paused, inert.

'The truth, the truth!' cried Peter, tossing his arms about—'Lo, from henceforth I will clamour for

it, rage for it, live for it, die for it! Three times have
I falsely sworn, and thus have I taken the full
measure of a Lie! Its breadth, its depth, its height,
its worth, its meaning, its result,—its crushing, suffo-
cating weight upon the soul! I know its nature—
'tis all hell in a word!—'tis a "yea" or "nay" on
which is balanced all eternity! I will no more of
it,—I will have truth,—the truth of men, the truth of
women,—no usurer shall be called honest,—no wanton
shall be called chaste, to please the humour of the
passing hour! No—no—I will have none of this—
but only truth!—the truth that is even as a shining
naked scimitar in the hand of God, glittering
horribly!—I, Peter, will declare it!—I who did swear
a lie three times, will speak the truth three thousand
times in reprisal of my sin! Weep, rave, tear thy
reverend hairs, unreverent Jew, thou, who as stiff-
necked righteous Pharisee didst practise cautious
virtue and self-seeking sanctity, and now through
unbelief art left most desolate! Would'st stake a
world upon thy daughter's honour?—Fie! 'tis dross!
—'tis common ware,—purchaseable for gold and
gewgaws! Lo, through this dazzling woman-snare,

born of thy blood, a God hath perished in Judæa!
His words have been rejected, — His message is
despised,—His human life hath been roughly torn
from Him by torture. Therefore upon Judæa shall
the curse be wrought through ages following endless
ages; and as the children of the house of Israel do
worship gold, even so shall gold be their damnation!
Like base slaves shall they toil for kings and counsellors; even as brutish beasts shall they be harnessed
to the wheels of work, and drag the heavier burdens
of the State beneath the whip and scourge,—despised and loathed, they shall labour for others, in
bondage. Scattered through many lands their
tribes shall be, and never more shall they be called
a nation! For ever and for ever shall the sinless
blood of the Messenger of God rest red upon
Judæa! — for ever and for ever from this day,
shall Israel be cast out from the promises of life
eternal,—a scorn and abomination in the sight of
Heaven!'

He paused, breathless, his hands uplifted as though
invoking doom. His rough cloak fell away from his
shoulders in almost regal folds, displaying his coarse

fisherman's dress beneath,—his figure seemed to grow taller and statelier, investing itself with a kind of mystic splendour in the shining radiance of the moon. Lifting his eyes to the stars twinkling like so many points of flame above him, he smiled, a wild and wondering smile.

'But the end is not yet!' he said—'There is a new terror and trembling, that doth threaten the land. For ye have murdered the Christ without slaying Him!—ye have forced Him to suffer death, but He is not dead! To-night He is buried,—shut down in the gloom of the grave,—what will ye do if the great stones laid above Him have no force to keep Him down?—what if the earth will not hold Him?— what if, after three days, as He said, He should rise to life again? I will aver nothing,—I will not again swear falsely,—I will shut my doubts and terrors in mine own soul and say no more, —but think of it, O ye unregenerate of Israel, what will ye do in the hour of trembling, if He, whom ye think dead, doth in very truth arise to life?'

His voice sank to a whisper,—he glanced about

him nervously,—then, as though seized by some sudden panic, he covered himself shudderingly up in his mantle so that his face could hardly be seen, and began to steal away cautiously on tip-toe.

'Think of it!' he repeated, looking back once at Iscariot with a wild stare — 'Perchance He may pardon Judas! Nay, I know nothing—I will swear nothing, — nevertheless 'twill be a strange world, — 'twill be an altogether different, marvellous world if He should keep His word, and after three days—no more, no less, He should arise again!'

And still moving as one in fear, shrouded in his cloak and stepping noiselessly, he turned abruptly and disappeared.

Iscariot gazed after him in mingled anger and perplexity.

'Is it some madman ye have brought hither?' he demanded — 'What manner of devil doth possess him?'

'The devil of a late remorse!' answered Melchior slowly — 'It doth move a man ofttimes to most

singular raving, and doth frequently inspire him to
singular deeds. The devil in this fisherman will
move the world!'

'Fisherman?' echoed Iscariot wonderingly—'Is he
no more than common?'

'No more than common,'—replied Melchior, his
eyes dilating singularly—'Common as—clay! Herein
will be his failure and his triumph. The scent of the
sea was round him at his birth,—from very boyhood
he hath contended with the raging winds and waters,
—so shall he yet contend with similarly warring
elements. No kings ever travelled from afar to kneel
before him in his cradle,—no Eastern sages proffered
gifts to honour him,—no angels sang anthems for
him in the sky,—these things were for the " Nazarene "
whom lately he denied, but whom he now will serve
most marvellously! But for the present, as the time
now goes, he is but Simon Peter, one of the fisher-
folk of Galilee, and lately a companion of thy dead
son Judas.'

A smothered groan escaped Iscariot's lips as his
eyes wandered to the extemporised bier on which the
corpse of Judas lay.

'Unhappy boy!' he murmured—'No wonder thou wert fanatic and wild, consorting with such friends as these!'

He went and stood by the covered body, and there, looking round towards his visitors with an air of sorrowful and resigned dignity, said,

'Ye will not take it ill of me, sirs, that I entreat ye now to leave me. The grief I have is almost too great to grasp,—my spirit is broken with mourning, and I am very weary. As for my daughter, thou, Barabbas, needest not that I should tell thee of the falsity of the slander brought against her by yon mad disciple of a mad reformer. Thou knowest her,—her innocence, her pride, her spotless virtue,—and to the friend thou hast with thee, thou wilt defend her honour and pure chastity. Thou hearest me?'

'I hear thee'—answered Barabbas in a choked voice—'And verily my whole heart aches for thee, Iscariot!'

The elder man looked at him keenly, and trembled.

'I thank thee, friend!' he then said quickly—

'Thou hast been guilty of heinous crimes, — but nevertheless I know thou hast manliness enough, and wilt, as far as lies within thy power, defend my child from scurrilous talk, such as this coarse-tongued Galilean fisherman may set current in the town.' He paused as though he were thinking deeply, — then beckoned Barabbas to approach him more closely. As his gesture was obeyed, he laid one hand on his son's veiled corpse and the other on Barabbas's arm.

'Understand me well!' he said in a fierce hoarse whisper—'If there were a grain of truth in that vile slander, I would kill Caiaphas!—yea, by this dead body of mine only son, I swear I would slay him before all the people in the very precincts of the Temple!'

In that one moment his face was terrible,—and the sombre eyes of Barabbas glittered a swift response to his thought. For a brief space the two men looked at each other steadily, and to Barabbas's excited fancy it seemed as if at the utterance of Iscariot's oath, the body of Judas trembled slightly underneath its heavy wrappings. One second, and the

sudden flash of furious comprehension that had
lighted their dark features as with fire, passed, and
the bereaved father bent his head in ceremonious
salutation.

'Farewell, sirs,'—he said, bidding Barabbas retreat
from him by a slight commanding sign — 'What
poor thanks a broken-hearted man can give are
yours for bringing home my dead. I will see ye
both again,—a few days hence,—when the bitter-
ness of grief is somewhat quelled, — when I am
stronger,— better fitted for reasonable speech,— but
now '——

He waved his hand in dismissal, and drawing his
mantle round him, sat down by his son's corpse, to
keep an hour's melancholy vigil.

Barabbas at once retired with Melchior, only
pausing on his way out to inquire of a passing
servant if Judith had recovered from her swoon. He
received an answer in the negative, given with tears
and doleful shaking of the head, and with a heavy
heart he left the house and passed into the moonlit
street. There, after walking a little way, Melchior
suddenly stopped, fixing his jewel - like contem-

plative eyes upon the brooding face of his companion.

'Dreamest thou, good ruffian, of the beauty of thy lost Judith?' he said—'I confess to thee I never saw a fairer woman! Even her sorrow doth enhance her loveliness.'

Barabbas shuddered.

'Why speak to me now of her beauty?' he demanded passionately—'Hath it not wrought sufficient havoc? Think of the dead Judas!'

'Truly I do think of him'—responded Melchior gravely—'All the world will think of him,—he will never be forgotten. Unhappy youth!—for history will make him answerable for sins that are not all his own. But the chronicles of men are not the chronicles of God,—and even Judas shall have justice in the end. Meantime'—and he smiled darkly—'knowest thou, good Barabbas, I am troubled by a singular presentiment? Poverty doth not oppress me,—nevertheless I swear unto thee, I would not in these days stake a penny piece upon the value of the life of Caiaphas! What thinkest thou?'

Barabbas stared at him, aghast, and breathing

quickly. And for a moment they remained so, gazing full at one another in the paling radiance of the sinking moon,—then walked on together, home-ward, in silence.

XXX

TOWARDS three o'clock in the dawn of the Jewish Sabbath, Judith Iscariot awoke from her heavy stupor of merciful unconsciousness. Opening her eyes, she gazed about her bewilderedly, and gradually recognised her surroundings. She was in her own room,—the casement was closed and lamps were burning, — and at the foot of her couch sat two of her waiting-women sunk in a profound slumber. Lifting herself cautiously upon her pillows, she looked at them wonderingly,—then peered round on all sides to see if any others were near. No,—there was no one,—only those two maids fast asleep. Gathering together her disordered garments, and twisting up her hair in a loose knot, she noiselessly arose, and stepping down from her couch, moved across

the room till she faced her mirror. There she
paused and smiled wildly at herself,—how strange
her eyes looked! . . . but how bright, how beautiful! The pearls Barabbas had given her long
ago, gleamed on her throat,—she fingered them
mechanically,—poor Barabbas!—certainly he had
loved her in days gone by. But since then,
many things had happened,—wonderful and confusing things,—and now there was only one thing
left to remember,—that after long absence and un-
kind estrangement Judas was once more at home.
Yes!—Judas was at home,—and she would go and
see him and talk to him, and clear up whatever
foolish misunderstanding there had been between
them. Her head swam giddily, and she felt a
feebleness in all her limbs,—shudders of icy cold
ran through her, followed by waves of heat that
sickened and suffocated her,—but she paid little
heed to these sensations, her one desire to see
Judas overpowering all physical uneasiness. She
fastened her white robe more securely about her
with a gold embroidered girdle, and catching sight
of her ornamental dagger where it lay on a table

close by, she attached it to her waist. Then
she glanced anxiously round at her two women,
—they still slept. Stepping heedfully on tip-toe,
she passed easily out of her room, for the door
had been left open for air, and there was only
the curtain at the archway to quietly lift and let
fall. Tottering a little as she walked, she glided
along the corridor, a white figure with a spectral
pale face and shining eyes,—she felt happy and
light-hearted,—almost she could have sung a merry
song, so singularly possessed by singular joy was
she. Reaching the open-air court she stopped,
gazing eagerly from side to side,—its dim quadrangle
was full of flickering lights and shadows, for the
moon had disappeared behind the frowning portico,
leaving but a silvery trail upon the sky to faintly
mark her recent passage among the stars. Everything was very still,—no living creature was visible
save a little downy owl that flew with a plaintive
cry in and out among the marble columns calling
to its mate with melancholy persistence. The
bereaved Iscariot, wearied out by grief, had but
just retired to snatch some sorely-needed rest ; and

the body of his hapless son, laid out beneath its
violet pall, possessed to itself the pallid hour of the
vanishing night and the coming morn. Judith's
softly sandalled feet made a delicate sound like
the pattering of falling leaves, as she moved somewhat unsteadily over the pavement, groping in the
air now and then with her hands as though she
were blind. Very soon her perplexed and wandering gaze found what she sought, — the suggestive
dark mass of drapery under which reposed all
that was mortal of her brother, the elder companion
and confidant of her childhood, who had loved her
with a tenderness 'passing that of women.' She
hurried her steps and almost ran,—and without any
hesitation or fear, turned back all the coverings
till the face and the whole form of the dead
Judas lay before her, stark and stiff, the rope
still fastened round the neck in dreadful witness
of the deed that had been done. Terribly beautiful he seemed in that pale semi - radiance of
the sky,—austerely grand,—with something of a
solemn scorn upon his features, and an amazing
world of passionate appeal in his upward gazing

eyes. 'Call ye me a traitor?' he mutely said to the watchful stars—'Lo, in the days to come, there shall be among professing saints many a worse than I!'

His sister looked at him curiously, with an expression of wild inquisitiveness,—but she neither wept nor trembled. A fixed idea was in her distracted brain,—undefined and fantastic,—but such as it was, she was bent upon it. With a strange triumph lighting up her eyes, she drew her jewelled dagger from its sheath, and with deft care cut asunder the rope round the throat of the corpse. As she pulled it cautiously away, the blood again oozed slowly forth from beneath the bruised skin,—this was mysterious and horrible, and terrified her a little, for she shuddered from head to foot. Anon she smiled,—and twisting the severed cord, stained and moist as it was, in and out the embroidered girdle at her own waist, she threw the dagger far from her into a corner of the quadrangle, and clapped her hands delightedly.

'Judas!' she exclaimed—'Lo! I have cut the cruel rope wherewith thou wast wounded,—now

thou canst breathe! Come!—rise up and speak
to me! Tell me all—I will believe all thy marvellous
histories! I will not say that thou art wrongly led,
—if thou wilt only smile again and speak, I will
pardon all thy foolish fancy for the teachings of the
"Nazarene." Thou knowest I would not drive thee
to despair,—I would not even willingly offend thee,
—I am thy little sister always who is dear to
thee. Judas—listen!—'Twas Caiaphas,—'twas the
high-priest himself who bade me tell thee to
betray thy Master, — and very rightly — for thy
mad prophet came in arms against our creed.
Why should'st thou turn rebellious and forsake
the faith of all our fathers? Come,—rise and
hear reason!'—and with the unnatural force of a
deepening frenzy, she bent down and partly raised
the corpse, staring at its fearful countenance with
mingled love and horror—' Why,—how thou lookest
at me!—with what cold unpiteous eyes? What
have I done to thee? Naught, save advise thee
wisely. As for Çaiaphas, — thou knowest not
Caiaphas—how much he can do for thee if thou
wilt show some fitting penitence'—here she broke

off with a kind of half-shriek,—the weight of the
dead body was too much for her and lurched
backward, dragging her with it,—she loosened her
arms from about it, and it straightway fell heavily
prone in its former position. She began to sob
childishly.

'Judas, Judas! Speak to me! Kiss me! I know
thou hearest me, and wilt not answer me for anger,
because this stranger out of Nazareth is dearer unto
thee than I!'

She waited in evident expectation of some response,—then, as the silence remained unbroken,
she began to play with the blood-stained rope at her
girdle.

'Ah well!' she sighed—'I am sorry thou art
sullen. Caiaphas would do great things for thee
if thou wert wise. Why should'st thou thus
grow desperate because of a traitor's death? What
manner of man was this much-marvelled-at
"Nazarene"? Naught but a workman's son, possessed of strange fanaticism! And shall so small
a thing sow rancour 'twixt us twain? Yet surely
I will humour thee if still to humour Him should

be thy fancy,—thou shalt have cross and crown made sacred an' thou wilt,—I can do no more in veriest kindness to appease thy wrath, — moreover thou dost maintain a useless churlishness, since thy "Nazarene" is dead, and cannot, even to please thee and amend thy sickness, rise again.'

Again she paused,—then commenced pacing to and fro in the shadowy court, looking about her vaguely. Presently spying her dagger where she had lately flung it in a corner, she picked it up and returned it to its sheath which still hung at her waist,—then she pulled down a long trail of climbing roses from the wall, and came to lay them on the breast of the irresponsive dead. As she approached, a sudden brilliant luminance affrighted her, — she started back, one hand involuntarily uplifted to shade her eyes. A Cross of light, deep red and dazzling as fire, hovered horizontally in the air immediately above the body of Judas, spreading its glowing rays outward on every side. She beheld it with amazement,— it glittered before her more brightly than the brightest sunbeams,—her fevered and wandering wits, not yet quite gone, recognised it as some miracle beyond human comprehension, and on the merest impulse she stretched forth her hands full of the just-gathered rose-clusters, in an effort to touch that lustrous, living flame. As she did so, a blood-like hue fell on her,—she seemed to be enveloped in a crimson mist that stained the whiteness of her garments and the fairness of her skin, and cast a ruddier tint than nature placed among the loosened tresses of her hair. The very roses that she held blushed into scarlet, while the waxen pallid features of the dead had for a little space a glow, as of returning life. For one or two minutes the mystic glory blazed,—then vanished, —leaving the air dull and heavy with a sense of loss. And Judith, standing paralysed with wonder, watched it disappear, and saw at the same time that a change had taken place in the aspect of her self-slain brother. The lips that had been drawn apart in the last choking agony of death were pressed together in a solemn smile,—the eyes that had stared aloft so fearfully were closed!

Seeing this, she began to weep and laugh hysteric-
ally, and flinging her rose-garland across the still
figure, she stooped and kissed that ice-cold smiling
mouth.

'Judas, Judas!' she said in smothered sobbing
accents — 'Now thou art gone to sleep, without
a word, — without a blessing, — thou wilt not
even look at me! Ah cruel! nevertheless I do
forgive thee, for surely thou art very weary,
else thou would'st not lie here so quietly beneath
the stars. I will let thee sleep on, — I will
not wake thee till the morning dawns. At full
daybreak I will come again and see that all is
well with thee, thou churlish one!—good-night!'
and she waved kisses to the dead man smil-
ingly with the tears blinding her eyes—'Good-
night, my brother! I will return soon, and
bring thee news—yea, I will bring thee pleas-
ing news of Caiaphas, . . . good-night! . . . sleep
well!'

And still waving fond and fantastic salutations,
she moved backward lightly on tip-toe step by step,
her gaze fixed to the last on the now composed and

beauteous face of the corpse,—then passing under the great portico, she noiselessly unfastened the gate, and wandered out in all her distracted and dishevelled beauty, into the silent streets of the city alone.

XXXI

THE full Sabbath morning broke in unclouded loveliness, and all the people of Jerusalem flocked to the gorgeous Temple on Mount Moriah to see and to be seen, and to render their formal thanks to the Most High Jehovah for their escape from all the threatening horrors of the previous day. Some there were who added to their prayers the unconscious blasphemy of asking God to pardon them for having allowed the 'Nazarene' to live even so long as He had done, seeing that His doctrines were entirely opposed to the spirit and the faith of the nation. Yet, all the same, a singular lack of fervour marked the solemn service, notwithstanding that in the popular opinion there was everything to be thankful for. The veil of the 'Holy of Holies,' rent in the midst, hung before the congregation as a

sinister reminder of the terrors of the past thunder-
storm, earthquake and deep darkness ; and the voice
of the high - priest Caiaphas grew wearily monotonous and indistinct long before the interminable
morning ritual was ended. Something seemed
missing, — there appeared to be no longer any
meaning in the usually imposing 'reading of the
law,' — there was a vacancy and dulness in the
whole ceremonial which left a cold and cheerless
impression upon the minds of all. When the crowd
poured itself forth again from the different gates,
many groups wended their way out of sheer curiosity
to the place where the 'Prophet of Nazareth' was
now ensepulchred, for the story of Joseph of
Arimathea's 'boldly' going to claim the body from
Pilate, and the instant vigilance of Caiaphas in
demanding that a watch should be set round the
tomb, had already been widely rumoured throughout
the city.

'We never had a more discreet and shrewd high-
priest,'—said one man, pausing in the stately King's
Portico to readjust the white linen covering on his
head more carefully before stepping out into the

unshaded heat and glare of the open road,—'He hath conducted this matter with rare wisdom, for surely the "Nazarene's" disciples would have stolen His body, rather than have Him proved a false blasphemer for the second time.'

'Ay, thou sayest truly!' answered his companion— 'And the whole crew of them are in Jerusalem at this time,—an ill-assorted dangerous rabble of the common folk of Galilee. Were I Caiaphas, I would find means of banishing these rascals from the city under pain of death.'

'One hath banished himself'—said the first speaker, 'Thou hast doubtless heard of the end of young Judas Iscariot?'

The other man nodded.

'Judas was mad,'—he said, 'Nothing in life could satisfy him,—he was ever prating of reforms and clamouring for truth. Such fellows are not fitted for the world.'

'Verily, he must himself have come to that conclusion'—remarked his friend with a grave smile, as he slowly descended the Temple steps,—'and so thinking, left the world with most determined will.

He was found hanging to the branch of a tree close by the garden of Gethsemane, and last night his body was borne home to his father's house.'

'But have ye heard no later news?' chimed in another man who had listened to the little conversation,—'Iscariot hath had another grief which hath driven him well-nigh distracted. He hath lost his chiefest treasure,—his pampered and too-much beloved daughter; and hath been to every neighbour seeking news of her and finding none. She hath left him in the night suddenly, and whither she hath gone no one can tell.'

By this time the group of gossips had multiplied, and startled wondering looks were exchanged among them all.

'His daughter!' echoed a bystander—'Surely 'tis not possible! The proud Judith? Wherefore should she have fled?'

'Who can say? She swooned last night at seeing her dead brother, and was carried unconscious to her bed. There her maidens watched her,—but in their watching, slept,—and when at last they wakened, she was gone.'

The listeners shook their heads dubiously as not knowing what to make of it ; and murmuring vague expressions of compassion for Iscariot, 'a worthy man and wealthy, who deserved not this affliction,' as they said, went slowly, talking as they went, homeward on their various ways.

Meanwhile, a considerable number of people had gathered together in morbid inquisitiveness round the guarded burial-place of the 'Nazarene.' It was situate in a wild and picturesque spot between two low hills, covered with burnt brown turf and bare of any foliage, and in itself presented the appearance of a cave deeply hollowed out in the natural rock. Rough attempts at outward adornment had been made in the piling-up of a few sparkling blocks of white granite in pyramidal form on the summit,— and these glittered just now like fine crystals in the light of the noonday sun. The square cutting that served as entrance to the tomb was entirely closed by a huge stone fitting exactly into the aperture,— and between this stone and the rock itself was twisted a perfect network of cords, sealed in about a hundred places with the great seal of the Sanhedrim

council. Round the sepulchre, on every side were
posted the watch, consisting of about fifteen soldiers
picked out from a special band of one hundred, and
headed by a formidable-looking centurion of muscular
build and grim visage, who, as the various groups of
idle spectators approached to look at the scene, eyed
them with fierce disfavour.

'By the gods!' he growled to one of his men—
'What a filthy and suspicious race are these cursëd
Jews! Lo you, how they sneak hither staring and
whispering! Who knows but they think we ourselves
may make away with the body of the man they
crucified yesterday! Worthily do they match their
high-priest in cautious cowardice! Never was such
a panic about a corpse before!'

And he tramped to and fro sullenly in front of
the tomb, his lance and helmet gleaming like silver
in the light, the while he kept his eyes obstinately
fixed on the ground, determined not to honour by
so much as a glance the scattered sightseers who
loitered aimlessly about, staring without knowing
what they stared at, but satisfied at any rate in their
own minds, that here assuredly there was no pretence

at keeping a watch,—these were real soldiers,—un-imaginative callous men for whom the 'Nazarene' was no more than a Jew reformer who had met his death by the ordinance of the law.

By and by, as the sun grew hotter, the little knots of people dispersed, repeating to one another as they sauntered along, the various wonderful stories told of the miracles worked by the dead 'Prophet out of Nazareth.'

'How boldly he faced Pilate!' said one.

'Ay!—and how grandly he died!'

'' Tis ever the way with such fellows as he '—declared another—'They run mad with much thinking, and death is nothing to them, for they believe that they will live again.'

So conversing, and alluding occasionally to the tragic incidents that had attended the sublime death - scene on Calvary, they strolled citywards, and only one of all the straggling spectators was left behind,—a man in the extreme of age, bent and feeble and wretchedly clad, who supported himself on a crutch, and lingered near the sepulchre, casting timorous and appealing glances at the men on guard.

Galbus, the centurion, observed him and frowned angrily.

'What doest thou here, thou Jew skeleton?' he demanded roughly—'Off with thee! Bring not thy sores and beggary into quarters with the soldiers of Rome!'

'Sir, sir'—faltered the old man anxiously—'I ask no alms. I do but seek thy merciful favour to let me lay my hands upon the stone of yonder tomb, . . . once, only once, good sir!—the little maid is sorely ailing, and methinks to touch the stone and pray there would surely heal her sickness'— He broke off, trembling all over, and stretching out his wrinkled hands wistfully.

Galbus stared contemptuously.

'What dost thou jabber of?' he asked—'The little maid?—what little maid? And what avails this touching of a stone? Thou'rt in thy dotage, man; get hence and cure thy wits,—'tis they that should be healed right speedily!'

'Sir!' cried the old man, almost weeping—'The little maid will die! Look you, good soldier, 'tis but a week agone that He who lies within that tomb, did take her in His arms and bless her ; she is but three years old and passing fair ! And now she hath been stricken with the fever, and methought could I but touch the stone of yonder sepulchre and say " Master, I pray thee heal the child," He, though He be dead, would hear and answer me. For He was ever pitiful for sorrow, and He was gentle with the little maid !'

Galbus flushed red,—there was a strange contraction in his throat of which he did not approve, and there was also a burning moisture in his eyes which was equally undesired. Something in this piteous old man's aspect, as well as the confiding simplicity of his faith touched the fierce soldier to an emotion of which he was ashamed. Raising his lance, he beckoned him nearer.

'Come hither, thou aged madman,' he said with affected roughness—'Keep close to me,—under my lifted lance, thou mayest lay hands upon the stone for one brief minute,—take heed thou break not the Sanhedrim seals!—And let thy prayer for thy little maid be of most short duration,—though take my word for it thou art a fool to think that a dead man hath ears to hearken thy petition. Nevertheless, come.'

Stumbling along and breathless with eagerness the old man obeyed. Close to the sacred sepulchre he came, Galbus guarding his every movement with vigilant eye,—and humbly kneeling down before the sealed stone he laid his aged hands upon it.

'Lord, if thou wilt,' he said—'Thou canst save the little maid! Say but the word and she is healed!'

One minute he knelt thus,—then he rose with a glad light in his dim old eyes.

'Most humbly do I thank thee, sir!' he said to the centurion, uncovering his white locks and bowing meekly—'May God reward thee for thy mercy unto me!'

Galbus gazed at him curiously from under his thick black eyebrows.

'Of what province art thou?'

'Sir, of Samaria.'

'And thinkest thou in very truth thou hast obtained a miracle from that tomb?'

'Sir, I know nothing of the secret ways divine.

But sure I am the little maid is saved. God be with thee, soldier! . . . God guide thy lance and evermore defend thee!'

And with many expressive salutations of gratitude he tottered away.

Galbus looked after him meditatively, till his thin raggedly-clothed figure had fluttered out of sight like a fluttering withered leaf,—then the grim Roman shook his head profoundly, pulled his beard, laughed, frowned, passed his hand across his eyes, and finally, having conquered whatever momentary soft emotion had possessed him, glanced about him severely and suspiciously to see that all his men were in their several places. The noonday heat and glare had compelled them to move into their tents, which were ranged all round the sepulchre in an even snowy ring,—and Galbus, seeing this, quickly followed their example, and himself retired within the shelter of his own particular pavilion. This was pitched directly opposite the stone which closed the mystic tomb,— and as the burly centurion sat down and lifted his helmet to wipe his hot face, he muttered an involuntary curse on the sultry and barren soil of Judæa, and wished himself heartily back in Rome.

'For this is a country of fools'—he soliloquised—'And worse still 'tis a country of cowards. These Jews were afraid of the " Nazarene " as they call Him, while He lived ; and now it seems they are more afraid of Him still when He is dead. Well, well ! 'tis a thing to laugh at,—a Roman will kill his enemy, true enough, but being killed he will salute the corpse and leave it to the gods without further fear or passion.'

At that moment an approaching stealthy step startled him. He sprang up, shouldered his lance and stood in the doorway of his tent expectant; a tall man muffled in a purple cloak confronted him,—it was Caiaphas who surveyed him austerely.

'Dost thou keep good watch, centurion?' he demanded.

'My vigilance hath never been questioned, sir,' responded Galbus stiffly.

Caiaphas waved his hand deprecatingly.

'I meant not to offend thee, soldier,—but there are knaves about, and I would have thee wary.'

He dropped his mantle, disclosing a face that was worn and haggard with suffering and want of sleep,—then, stepping close up to the sepulchre, he narrowly examined all the seals upon the stone. They were as he had left them on the previous evening, untouched, unbroken.

'Hast thou heard any sound?' he asked in a whisper. Galbus stared.

'From within yonder?' he said, pointing with his lance at the tomb—'Nay!—never have I heard voice proceed from any dead man yet.'

Caiaphas forced a smile,—nevertheless he bent his ear against the stone and listened.

'What of the night?' he queried anxiously—'Were ye interrupted in your first watch?'

'By the baying of dogs at the moon, and the hooting of owls only'—replied Galbus disdainfully,—'And such interruptions albeit distasteful, are not to be controlled.'

'I meant not these things'—said Caiaphas, turning upon him vexedly—'I thought the women might have lingered, making lamentation'——

'Women have little chance where I am,' growled

Galbus,—'True, they did linger till I sent them off.
Yet I treated them with kindness, for they were weeping
sorely, foolish souls,—the sight of death doth ever
move them strangely,—and 'twas a passing beauteous
corpse o'er which they made their useless outcry.
Nevertheless I am not a man to find consolements for
such grief,—I bade them mourn at home ;—the tears
of women do provoke me more than blows.'

Caiaphas stood lost in thought,—anon he stooped
again to listen at the sealed-up door of the sepulchre.
Galbus, watching him, laughed.

' By the gods, sir,' he said—' One would think thou
wert the chief believer in the dead man's boast that
he would rise again! What hearest thou? Prithee
say!—a message from the grave would be rare
news!'

Caiaphas deigned no reply. Muffling himself again
in his mantle, he asked—

' When does the watch change?'

'In an hour's time,' replied Galbus—'Then I,
together with my men, rest for a space,—in such
heat as this, rest is deserved.'

' And when dost thou return again?'

'To-night at moonrise.'

'To-night at moonrise!' echoed Caiaphas thoughtfully. 'Mark my words, Galbus, watch thy men and
guard thyself from sleeping. To-night use double
vigilance!—for when to-night is past, then fears are
past,—and when to-morrow's sun doth shine, and he,
the "Nazarene," is proved again a false blasphemer
to the people, then will all watching end. Thou wilt
be well rewarded,—watch, I say, to-night!—far more
to-night than any hour of to-day! Thou hearest
me?'

Galbus nodded.

'I have heard much of the truth and circumspect-
ness of the soldiery of Rome'—proceeded Caiaphas,
smiling darkly—'And specially of warriors like thee,
who have the mastery of a hundred men, from which
this present watch is chosen. Take heed therefore
to do thy calling and thy country justice,—so shall
thy name be carried on the wings of praise to Cæsar.
Fare-thee-well!'

He moved away—then paused, listening doubt-
fully, — with head turned back over his shoulder
towards the tomb.

'Art thou sure thou hast heard nothing?' he asked again.

Galbus lost patience.

'By the great name of the Emperor I serve, and by the lance I carry,' he exclaimed, striking his heel on the ground, 'I swear to thee, priest, nothing—nothing!'

'Thou hast hot blood, soldier'—returned Caiaphas sedately—'Beware lest it lead thee into error!'

And he paced slowly down the dusty road and disappeared. Galbus watched his retreating form with an irrepressible disgust written on every feature of his face. One of his men approached him.

''Twas the Jewish high-priest that spoke with thee?'

'Ay, 'twas even he'—he responded briefly—'Either I choke in his presence, or the dust kicked up by his holy sandals hath filled me with a surpassing thirst. Fetch me a cup of wine.'

The man obeyed, getting the required beverage out of the provision tent.

'Ah, that washes the foul taste of the Jew out
of my mouth,'—said Galbus, drinking heartily—
'Methinks our Emperor hath got a beggarly
province here in Judæa. Why, if history have
any truth in it, 'tis the custom of this people
to be conquered and sold into slavery. I believe
of all my hundred, thou dost know thy lessons
best, Vorsinius,—have not these Jews been always
slaves?'

Vorsinius, a young soldier with a fair intelligent
countenance, smiled.

'I would not say so much as that, good Galbus,'
he replied modestly—'but methinks they have never
been heroes.'

'No,—nor will they ever be,' said Galbus, draining
his cup and shaking the dregs out on the ground—
'Such names as hero and Jew, consort not well
together. What other nation in the world than
this one would insist on having a watch set
round a tomb lest perchance a dead man should
rise!'

He laughed, and the good-humoured Vorsinius
laughed with him. Then they resumed their

respective posts, and moved no more till in an hour's time the watch was changed. But save for the clanking of armour as one party of soldiers marched away into the city, and the other detachment took its place, the deep and solemn silence round the sealed Sepulchre remained unbroken.

XXXII

MEANWHILE Barabbas, sitting with his friend
Melchior in the best room of the inn where
that mysterious personage had his lodging, was
endeavouring to express his thanks for the free and
ungrudging hospitality that had been afforded him.
He had supped well, slept well, and breakfasted
well, and all at the cost and care of this new acquaintance with whom, as might be said, he was barely
acquainted, — moreover the very garments he wore
were Melchior's, and not his own.

'If thou seekest a man to work, I will work for
thee'—he said now, fixing his large bold black eyes
anxiously on the dark enigmatical face of his voluntary patron,—'But unless thou canst make use of
my strength in service, I can never repay thee. I
have no kinsfolk in the world,—mother and father

are dead long since, and well for them that it is so, for I should have doubtless been their chief affliction. Once I could make a boast of honesty,—I worked for the merchant Shadeen, and though I weighed out priceless gems and golden ingots, I never robbed him by so much as a diamond chip until—until the last temptation. If thou wilt ask him, he will I know say this of me—for he was sorrier for my sin than I had heart to be. I have some little knowledge of books and old philosophies,—and formerly I had the gift of fluent speech,—but whatsoever I might have been, I am not now,—my hands are stained with blood and theft,—and though the people set me free, full well I know I am an outcast from true liberty. Nevertheless thou hast fed me, housed me, clothed me, and told me many wise and wondrous things,— wherefore out of gratefulness, which I lack not, and bounden duty, I am fain to serve thee and repay thee, if thou wilt only teach me how.'

Melchior, leaning back on a low window-seat, surveyed him placidly from under his half-closed eyelids, a faint smile on his handsome mouth.

'Friend Barabbas,' he responded lazily, 'thou owest me nothing—on the contrary, 'tis I that owe thee much. Thou art a type of man,—even as I also am a type of man,—and I have derived much benefit from a study of thy complex parts,—more benefit perchance than is discovered in the "old philosophies" wherewith thou fanciest thou art familiar. Mark thou the difference betwixt us!—though seemingly our composition is the same dull mortal clay. Thou art poor,—thou hast but yester morn left prison, naked and ashamed,—I am rich, not by the gifts of men, which things I spurn, or by the leavings of the dead, but by the work of mine own brain, man's only honest breadwinner. I have never found my way to prison, as I despise all roads that lead one thither. They are foul,—therefore, loving cleanness, I tread not in them. Thou, made animal man, and ignorant of the motive power of brain that masters matter, didst at the bidding of mere fleshly lust resign thine honour for a woman's sake,—I, made intelligent man, do keep my honour for my own sake, and for the carrying out of higher laws which I perceive exist. Nevertheless thou art truer man than I. Thou art

II.—15

the type of sheer brute manhood, against which
Divine Spirit for ever contends.'

He paused ;—and lifting his head from its recum-
bent position, smiled again.

'What wilt thou do for me, Barabbas?' he continued lightly—'Draw water, till the soil, shake my
garments free from dust, or other such slavish service?
Go to! I would not have thee spoil thy future!
Take my advice and journey thou to Rome,—I'll fill
thy pouch with coin,—settle thyself as usurer there
and lend out gold to Cæsar! Lend it freely, with
monstrous interest accumulating, for the use of the
Imperial whims, battles, buildings, and wantons! So
get thee rich and live honourably,—none will ask of
thee—"wert thou thief?"—"wert thou murderer?"
No!—for the Emperor will kiss thy sandal and put
on thee his choicest robe,—and all thou hast to do is
to keep his name upon thy books and never let it go.
"Ave Cæsar Imperator" is the keynote of the Roman
shouting — but Cæsar's whisper in thine ear will
have more meaning — "Hail, Barabbas, King of the
Jews! rich Barabbas, who doth lend me money,—
noble Barabbas, who willingly reneweth bills, —

powerful Barabbas, who doth hold the throne and dynasty by a signature!"

He laughed, the while his companion stared at him fascinated and half afraid.

'Or,' pursued Melchior, 'wilt thou by preference make friends with frenzied Peter, and join the disciples of the "Nazarene"?'

'Not with Peter—no!' exclaimed Barabbas in haste,—'I like him not,—he is not certain of his faith! And of the other men who came from Galilee I know naught, save that they all forsook their Master. I would have followed the "Nazarene" Himself into the blackest hell!—but His followers are coward mortals and He'——

'Was Divine, thinkest thou?' asked Melchior, fixing upon him a look of searching gravity.

Barabbas met his gaze steadily for a moment, then his own eyes fell and he sighed deeply.

'I know not what to think,' he confessed at last. 'When I first beheld Him, He did in very truth seem all Divine!—then,—the glory vanished, and only a poor patient suffering Man stood there, where I, faint from the prison famine and distraught of fancy,

imagined I had seen an Angel! Then when He died
—ah then, my soul was shaken!—for to the very last
I hoped against all hope,—surely, I said, a God can
never die! And now, if thou wilt have the truth, I
judge Him as a martyred Man,—of glorious beauty,
of heroic character,—one worthy to follow, to love, to
serve ; . . . but . . . if He had been indeed a God,
He could not thus have died!'

Melchior leaned forward, resting his chin on one
hand and studying him curiously.

'Knowest thou, excellent Barabbas, what is this
death?' he asked—'Among the "old philosophies"
thou readest, hast mastered aught concerning its true
nature?'

'All men know what it is;'—replied Barabbas
drearily—'A choking of the breath,—a blindness of
the eyes,—darkness, silence, and an end!'

'Nay, not an end, but a beginning!' said Melchior,
rising and confronting him, his eyes flashing with
enthusiasm — 'That choking of the breath,—that
blindness of the eyes—these are the throes of birth,
not death! Even as the new-born child struggles for
air, and cannot too suddenly endure the full unshaded

light of day,—so does the new-born soul that
struggles forth from out its fleshly womb, fight gasp-
ingly for strength to take its first deep breathings-in
of living glory! A darkness and a silence, sayest
thou? Not so!—a radiance and a music!—a wondrous clamour of the angels' voices ringing out
melodies aloft like harps in tune! And of the spirit
lately parted from the earth, they ask—"What
bringest thou? What message dost thou bear?
Hast thou made the sad world happier, wiser, fairer?"
And over all, the deathless Voice of Marvel thunders ;
"Soul of a man! What hast thou done?" And
that great question must be met and answered,—and
no Lie will serve!'

Barabbas gazed at him, awed, but incredulous.

'This is the faith of Egypt?' he asked.

Melchior eyed him with a touch of scorn.

'The faith of Egypt!' he echoed—''Tis not faith,
'tis knowledge!—Knowledge gained through faith!
'Tis no more of Egypt than of any land,—'tis a truth,
and as a truth is universal,—a truth the "Nazarene"
was born to make most manifest. The world is never
ripe for truth,—how should it be, so long as it is well

content to build its business and its social life on
lies !'

He paused, and recovering from his momentary
excitement, went on in his coldest and most satirical
tone—

' Worthy Barabbas, thou, like the world, art most
unfitted for the simplest learning, despite thine "old
philosophies." Such common facts as that there are
millions upon millions of eternal worlds, and millions
upon millions of eternal forms of life, would but con-
fuse thy brain and puzzle it. Thou art a mass of
matter, unpermeated by the fires of the spirit,—and
were I to tell thee that the " Nazarene " has " died "
according to the common word, only to prove there
is no death at all, thy barbarous mind would be most
sore perplexed and troubled. Thou hast not yet
obtained the mastery of this planet's laws,—thou'rt
brute man merely,—though now, methinks thou'rt
more like some fierce tiger disappointed of its mate,
for thou canst not wed thy Judith '——

Barabbas interrupted him with a fierce gesture.

' I would not wed her—now !'

' No ? Thou would'st rather murder Caiaphas ?'

Barabbas shuddered. His black brows met in a close frown,—his lips were pressed together hard, and his eyes were almost hidden under their brooding lids.

'I have already blood upon my hands,' he muttered, 'And the man I killed—Gabrias—was innocent,— my God!—innocent as a dove compared to this wolfish priest who works his evil will by treachery and cunning. Nevertheless since I beheld the "Nazarene"'——

'Why should the "Nazarene" affect thee?' asked Melchior placidly—'A martyred Man, thou sayest— no more,—thou canst be sorry for Him, as for many another—and forget.'

Barabbas lifted his eyes.

'I cannot take a human life again,' he said solemnly, his voice trembling a little—'since I have looked upon His face!'

Melchior was silent.

A long pause ensued,—then Barabbas resumed in calmer tones—

'If thou wilt give me leave, I will go forth and ask for news of old Iscariot,—and of his daughter,—for though I may not, would not wed her, because my own great sins—and hers—have set up an everlasting barrier between us, I love her, Heaven help me, still. I have slept late and heard nothing,—wherefore to ease my mind concerning her, I will inquire how she fares. I would I could forget the face of the dead Judas!'

A tremor ran through him, and he moved restlessly.

''Twas a face to be remembered'—said Melchior meditatively—'Set in the solemn shadows of the trees, 'twas a pale warning to the world! Nevertheless, despite its frozen tragedy, it was not all despair. Remorse was written in its staring eyes,—remorse,—repentance; and for true repentance, God hath but one reply—pity, and pardon!'

'Thinkest thou in very truth his sin will be forgiven?' exclaimed Barabbas eagerly.

'Not by the world that drove him to that sin's committal!'—answered Melchior bitterly—'The world that hunts men down to desperation, hath no pity for the desperate. But God's love never falters, —even the trembling soul of Judas may find shelter in that love!'

His voice grew very sweet and grave,—and a sudden moisture dimmed Barabbas's eyes.

'Thy words do comfort me,' he murmured huskily, ashamed of his emotion—'albeit I have been told that God is ever a God of vengeance. But Judas was so young, . . . and Judith'— He broke off—then added whisperingly—'I forgot—he bled at her touch! —'twas horrible—horrible,—that stain of blood on her white fingers!'

Melchior said nothing, and Barabbas, after a minute or two, rose up to go out.

'I must breathe the air'—he said abruptly—'The heat within the house doth choke me. I will ask where the "Nazarene" is buried and go thither.'

'Why?' inquired Melchior—'Since thou believest not in Him, what is He to thee?'

'I cannot tell'—answered Barabbas slowly— 'Something there is that draws me to the thought of Him, but what it is I cannot yet discover. If I believe not in Him as a God, 'tis because what I hear of Him doth pass all human understanding. Even what thou hast briefly told me doth utterly confound all reason,—the miracle of His birth when

His mother Mary was a virgin,—how can I credit this? 'Tis madness ; and my soul rejects that which I cannot comprehend.'

'Did I not tell thee what a type thou wert and art?' said Melchior—'A type of man unspiritualised, and therefore only half instructed. If thou rejectest what thou canst not comprehend, thou must reject the whole wide working of the universe! " *Where wast thou,*" God said unto His servant Job, "*when I laid the foundations of the earth? Declare if thou hast understanding? . . . Hast thou commanded the morning since thy days?*" Alas, most profound and reasonable Barabbas!—if thou dost wait till thou canst "comprehend" the mysteries of the Divine Will, thou wilt need to grope through æons upon æons of eternal wonder, living a thinking life through all, and even then not reach the inner secret. Comprehendest thou how the light finds its sure way to the dry seed in the depths of earth and causes it to fructify?—or how, imprisoning itself within drops of water and grains of dust, it doth change these things of ordinary matter into diamonds which queens covet? Thou art not able to "comprehend" these simplest facts of simple nature,—and nature being but the outward reflex of God's thought, how should'st thou understand the workings of His interior Spirit which is Himself in all? Whether He create a world, or breathe the living Essence of His own Divinity into aerial atoms to be absorbed in flesh and blood, and born as Man of virginal Woman, He hath the power supreme to do such things, if such be His great pleasure. Talkest thou of miracles?—thou art thyself a miracle, —thou livest in a miracle,—the whole world is a miracle, and exists in spite of thee! Go thy ways, man; search out truth in thine own fashion; but if it should elude thee, blame not the truth which ever is, but thine own witlessness which cannot grasp it!'

Barabbas stood silent, — strangely moved and startled by the broadness of his new friend's theories.

'I would I could believe in such a God as thou dost picture!' he said softly—'One who doth indeed love us, and whom we could love!'

He paused and sighed; — then on a sudden impulse, approached Melchior and taking his hand, kissed it.

'I know not who thou art,' he said—'but thy words are brave and bold, and to me thou hast been more than generous. Thou must consider me thy servant,—for as I told thee, I have no other means of paying back the debt I owe thee. Suffer me therefore to attend thee,—at least till I find ways of work,—shall this be so?'

Melchior smiled.

'Thou shalt do even as thou wilt, Barabbas, albeit I do not need attendance. Myself hath been my bodyguard for years,—and I have never found a more discreet and faithful confidant! Nevertheless, to satisfy thy sudden-tender conscience, I will accept thy service.'

A look of relief that was almost happiness, lightened Barabbas's dark features, giving them a certain nobleness and beauty.

'I thank thee!' he said simply—'Can I do aught now for thee within the city?'

'Thou canst bring me news!'—returned Melchior, fixing his eyes upon him steadily—'There may be some of highest import. And mark me!—if thou dost visit the tomb of the "Nazarene," take heed,—thou wilt find it strongly guarded. Quarrel not with those who watch, lest thou should'st be accused of some conspiracy to steal the corpse,—the Jewish priests are yet in terror, for the "Nazarene" did swear that on the "third day," that is, to-morrow,— remember, to-morrow!—He would rise again.'

Barabbas stopped in the very act of leaving the room, and turning on the threshold exclaimed,

'Impossible! Thou dost echo the last night's frenzy of Peter! Rise, living, from the grave? Impossible! He cannot!'

Melchior looked full at him.

'If Death be death, why truly He cannot;'—he responded,—'But if Death be Life, why then He can!'

END OF VOLUME II.

MORRISON AND GIBB, PRINTERS, EDINBURGH.

www.ingramcontent.com/pod-product-compliance
Lightning Source LLC
Chambersburg PA
CBHW020119030726
47498CB00006B/2188